Arachnid
Aditya Modak

Ukiyoto Publishing

All global publishing rights are held by

Ukiyoto Publishing
Published in 2021

Content Copyright © Aditya Modak
ISBN 9789364949385

All rights reserved.
No part of this publication may be reproduced, transmitted, or stored in a retrieval system, in any form by any means, electronic, mechanical, photocopying, recording or otherwise, without the prior permission of the publisher.

The moral rights of the author have been asserted.

This is a work of fiction. Names, characters, businesses, places, events, locales, and incidents are either the products of the author's imagination or used in a fictitious manner. Any resemblance to actual persons, living or dead, or actual events is purely coincidental.

This book is sold subject to the condition that it shall not by way of trade or otherwise, be lent, resold, hired out or otherwise circulated, without the publisher's prior consent, in any form of binding or cover other than that in which it is published.

Dedicated to Bidur Debnath

CONTENTS

Chapter 1	1
Chapter 2	17
Chapter 3	30
Chapter 4	33
Chapter 5	40
Chapter 6	60
About the Author	***122***

"God has given you one face, and you make yourselves another."
— William Shakespeare,
Hamlet

"God is dead."
— Friedrich Nietzsche,
The Gay Science

Chapter 1

The light from the laptop's LCD screen illuminated Jay's gas-mask covered face with a drab, unnatural glow. Fingers frozen on the keyboard, and eyes peering into the distance, Jayaraj "Jay" Mukherjee was sitting at the desk of his little office room. He had been sitting that way for quite some time now. He was so preoccupied with his thoughts that he could not tell when his documents had slipped from his lap onto the dusty floor. A second person, if they entered the room at that moment, would have assumed that Jay was lost in a daydream, or that he had turned into a statue. But the office room could never be an ideal place for daydreaming. Not only because it was clumsy and stuffy, but also because it was an **office room**. With all the folders, files, devices, responsibilities and noises from the machines and the city, it was anything but a daydream-friendly environment. It was also way too crude a place for accommodating a statue. And more importantly than either of that, there was no time. No time for daydreaming; no time for turning into a statue.

It was fourteen o'clock in the afternoon, the one hundred and seventy-first day of the year. The weather forecast in the morning had predicted a "hot and humid day." Most of the time, the forecast proved to be wrong, but unfortunately for Jay, it was one of those rare occasions where the theatrical weatherman's prediction had come true. It was not the kind of weather that facilitated the constant movement of hands sifting through papers, and fingers tapping on the keyboard in a dingy little office room with a damaged air conditioner. A table fan had been assigned to work as a substitute until the air conditioner recovered, but it was not quite efficient at the job. The monotonous squeaking of its blades was the only sign of its presence.

But there was nothing he could do about it, as the superintendent had already instructed Jay to "manage with this" until the electrician fixed the air conditioner.

It had been over seven days but there was no sign of the electrician. What really irked Jay was that out of all the chambers in the post office, his was the only one with a damaged air conditioner. But he still had to keep working. Would they throw in an additional thousand world dollars to his salary for his troubles?

No. *Of course not.*

That was not how the Federation worked, and Jay was well aware of that. Once a person joined the system, they would become a part of it; they would have to go with the flow. Complaining, questioning, resisting, and protesting were deemed "unprofessional conduct." One had to keep one's grievances to oneself in order to retain one's earmarked position or rank in the system. After all, every single person working for the

Federation was just another spoke on a gigantic wheel that kept rotating perpetually. In this system, there was a replacement for everything in order to ensure continuity. Everybody and everything there could be replaced, similar to the way the air conditioner was replaced by the table fan.

Therefore, Jay had to make do with this arrangement. Opening the windows, in this case, was out of the question since the office sat in the heart of the city. People here kept their doors and windows closed for breathing fresh air. Here the children played indoors, birds were kept in cages, and synthetic plants were grown in little plastic tubs kept in the little balconies that looked out to the rushing roads, where the people and the automobiles appeared like puny toys and insects.

Drops of sweat clung on to Jay's forehead as he sat in his squalid office chamber in the red-hot summer afternoon. He had to submit a report to the superintendent by eighteen o'clock. There were a lot of pages to be filled up, and a lot of data to be crosschecked, with less than four hours in hand.

But Jay was not working.

His laptop screen had turned black. His files were on the floor.

He was staring at the dirty, discoloured wall before him.

Several spots, from where the dull pink paint had fallen off, marred the wall with puffy flakes and white blotches. Ensconced in the middle of one such blotch was the cause of Jay's distraction.

A tiny, appalling creature with eight legs.

A spider.

There was nothing extraordinary about the spider. It was one of those brown, emaciated house spiders, which were very frequently encountered indoors. But it had managed to grab Jay's attention for a reason.

A special reason.

The spider had taken him to a different place. Jay had allowed himself to be taken there, leaving the chamber and the office and the clamour of the bustling city behind him.

He swam across the ocean of time, revisiting a place amongst memories that were fading like the corners of a decrepit photograph.

(*A familiar place*)

On a Sunday evening

(*when Sundays used to be holidays*)

twenty-eight years ago.

(*when wearing masks was an option*)

He could identify the aroma of cardamom, cinnamon, ginger, and tea leaves in the air. His mother was in the kitchen. He heard the coda of a musical composition, which he could not recognize. His father was in the living room, playing his prized records.

The eight-year-old Jay had just come back home from the playground. He had been playing cricket with his friends.

Unbeknownst to the child, in eight years, cricket would retire as a sport; in ten years, a condominium would stand in the middle of the playground; in fifteen years, music records would become practically unaffordable; in twenty-two years, his parents would be dead; and throughout the course of the next twenty-eight years, time and time again, he would keep looking back at this day.

Something crucial was about to happen: a momentous event that would etch itself on Jay's memory forever.

Jumping on his toes, Jay kicked off his shoes, and sprinted for the bathroom. The game had gotten too intense for a pee break.

His urgency to urinate was increasing with every step. By the time he reached the bathroom door, he was ready to burst. The switchboard outside the bathroom was still out of Jay's reach. He had to jump every time to get the tip of his finger on the lower end of the switch. And it always required more than just one jump. His personal record was six. But he could not risk making such movements now.

So he went in without turning on the light.

The record player in the living room started to play the recognizable fanfare to Strauss's *Also sprach Zarathustra*.

(*Did it, really?*)

It was not dark yet. The waning gleam of dusk was entering into the bathroom through the ventilator.

Jay lifted the lid of the commode

(*what-*)

and froze on the spot.

A severed hand was laid on the rim.

A brown, tattooed hand with long, curved, skeletal fingers.

But so many fingers?

No. Not fingers.

They were legs.

It took Jay a moment to realise that it was not a hand, but an animal.

A spider.

It was unlike any other spider he had ever seen before. In fact, it was unlike *anything* he had ever seen before.

It was huge – so much so that its features could be made out clearly: the numerous eyes, the moving jaws, the eight legs, the hairy body...

The last light of the day revealed a design, which Jay had mistaken as a tattoo, on the spider's enormously bloated body.

The design resembled something.

Two wide-open eyes. Two flared nostrils. A gaping mouth.

A face. A human face.

Jay felt a warm and wet stream running down his legs.

The music coming from the living room – the pounding timpani – mingled with his thumping heart and the sounds of the roaring city.

He knew that he had to scream. He *had* to, but his jaws were locked tight. He felt like running, but he could not do that either. His legs, wet with urine, refused to move. All he could do was stand and stare. And wait. But wait for what?

The spectacle before his eyes turned into a swirl of colours.

The brightness of the light and the volume of the music were gradually turned down, until darkness and silence wrapped him up.

When he opened his eyes, he saw a face hovering above him. It was the same face he had seen on the spider's back. Startled, he sat up. Before he could react any further, the features of the face rapidly twisted into a more "human" form.

"It's okay, it's okay," said the owner of the face: a man.

8 Arachnid

Jay felt his mother's arms around him.

She covered his face with kisses.

"What happened, *baba*?" she asked.

He could not answer immediately. It took him a few seconds to process whatever was going on.

He was on his bed, completely naked. He quickly pulled the bed sheets over himself.

"I am Doctor Uncle," the unknown man said, putting his hand on Jay's head. "How are you feeling now?"

Unsure of what to say, Jay nodded. That was all he could do at the moment.

"What happened in the bathroom? Did you fall down?" his father asked.

The bathroom.

That brought back a vivid image of the hellish creature, and the face on its back. Jay shuddered. He tried to speak, but his lips were still sealed with glue.

(sealed with the spider's web.)

It was then revealed that Jay had developed arachnophobia. It was strange because he had never shown any fear of spiders before. In fact, he had watched a television documentary on spiders just fourteen days ago, and it did not unnerve him at all.

"You never know when the fear shows up," Doctor Uncle said. "It doesn't require a build-up. There is no foreshadowing. It just happens."

He referred Jay to a psychiatrist, an old man with snow-white hair, who very confidently asserted that the fear would be totally gone within two days.

Looking at the form Jay had filled up, the old psychiatrist, Dr Ray, said, "Spider-Man is your favourite superhero?"

Jay nodded.

"Then why are you afraid of spiders? What would Spider-Man say?"

"Nothing," Jay said to himself. "He doesn't exist. I'm not stupid."

But he only shrugged, because he knew that nobody liked a wisecracker.

Also, he was not in a position to be making smart remarks. *Being a smartass and afraid of spiders!* Anyway, he knew he did not have to worry about Spider-Man. He would not have to deal with him. But he definitely would have to deal with spiders.

Lots and lots of spiders.

"Friendly Neighbourhood Spider-Man." Unfriendly neighbourhood Spider.

The first session was spent binge watching video clips of spiders. Jay's skin crawled as he watched them. He felt as if little spiders were running beneath his skin. But that was disgust, not fear. None of the spiders had a screaming human face on its back.

By the time the fourth video clip began, that creepy feeling had vanished.

However, a different feeling had taken its place. It was a wet, trickling, warm feeling on his legs; and it was mixed with hatred, embarrassment, shame, and disgust. But he did not say that to the psychiatrist. Some things were better left unsaid.

At the end of the first session, without any warning, the psychiatrist pulled out a huge rubber spider from under his desk. Jay squirmed in his seat. The thing looked real for a moment.

"How stupid!" Jay reprimanded himself for reacting that way.

The spider had a blue, fat body, green, wriggly legs, and a little black head with two big, googly eyes.

Putting the spider on the desk in front of Jay, the psychiatrist pressed its swollen midriff. It made a funny squeak.

"Do you like it?" he asked.

"I don't know," Jay said.

"Here, touch it."

Jay touched the spider's rubber body, feeling the tiny ridges and spines.

It's just a toy, he thought.

A parody of the real thing could never invoke the desired results in the human psyche, and even the eight-year-old Jay understood that.

Why'd I be afraid of a toy?

But in the second session, Dr Ray brought in a little cardboard box, and asked Jay to look inside.

Jay had already guessed what was in there.

Sitting at the corner of the empty box, was a tiny spider.

And it was not a toy this time. It was a real, live spider.

Jay felt a warm stream running down his legs. He looked down to check if he had actually wet himself again.

"See," Dr Ray said, putting his hand inside the box. "It's harmless."

Waving its little arm-like pedipalps in the air, the spider huddled up in a corner of the box.

"There's no reason to be afraid of them. They're friendly little animals. Now you put your hand in there," the psychiatrist said.

"Do I have to?"

"You have to face your fears," the old psychiatrist said. "You can't run away from them. Wait. Allow this music to accompany your feet."

He switched on the music player, from which emerged the familiar fanfare of *Also sprach Zarathustra*.

(Did it, really?)

Very slowly, Jay extended his shaky hand towards the box. The spider was sitting still in the corner.

What's it thinking? "Stupid humans!"

Closing his eyes, and holding his breath, Jay put his hand inside the box.

The diagnosis was given that very afternoon.

Jay was cured.

His phobia went away as strangely as it had come. But Jay did not consider the psychiatric sessions to be of any help. He believed that he was never really scared of spiders. It was only *that creature* he had seen in the bathroom. It had triggered something in him.

The "creature," however, was not found in the bathroom, or anywhere else in his house. Despite his father's assurances, Jay spent the rest of his time in that house dreading another altercation. Never again did he enter the bathroom without turning on the lights first. Although he did not run into the spider, or that face ever again, the warm wetness he had felt trickling down his legs that evening continued to return every time he came across a spider.

And the feeling returned once again, twenty-eight years later, on a steaming afternoon, as Jay stared at a spider on the wall of his office room.

"I wonder what happened to *that* spider," he thought. "We never found it anywhere. Is it possible that it never really existed? Was it something that my mind had made up?"

The last question could not be disregarded. Jay knew that the human brain tricked the mind to conjure such events of the past that never really took place. For instance, the bloody "Battle of the Himalayas," which had shaken the world, and had become a matter of lengthy, heated discussions and debates all over the press, was later proven by the Federation to be the symptom of a mass psychogenic illness. So it was not improbable for an eight-year-old to conjure such a spectre as a manifestation of his fears.

Another big question mark was the composition he always associated with that incident: Richard Strauss's *Also sprach Zarathustra*. More precisely, the fanfare, "Sunrise."

His father had had a huge collection of jazz, rock, and classical music albums, and Jay grew up listening to them. In spite of the growing popularity of factory music, he enjoyed the oldies. But the enjoyment was short-lived.

All the music files and videos were taken down from the internet after its privatization. They were burned into DVDs, and sold at mind boggling prices. Only the lucky ones who still had the MP3 files stored in their hard drives could still listen to music for free. But after the Trojan-50 e-pandemic, almost every single one of those music files disappeared. The Federation later "requisitioned " Jay's father's coveted collection for archiving them in the confidential vaults of the Academy of Arts.

The only remaining option was to listen to contemporary factory music. Not only did Jay find it unbearable, but he also never understood how the "music engineers" simply recorded noises from the industries, labelled them as music, and made a career out of it. But he did not have to think about it for very long. Due to the steady rise in the price of music albums, the discontinuation of free music streaming services, and the shortage of time, he could not listen to music anymore.

And thus, the common people were left with only the memories of music.

But why Also sprach Zarathustra*?*

Was it because that was one of the few classical music pieces he had actually remembered?

It did not really matter. Even if the inclusion of the music were a figment of his imagination, it would still not alter the fact that he had to seek counselling for arachnophobia. And it was a fact that he had kept to himself all these years. Not even his wife, Sunita, knew about it. Everybody else who did: his parents, the old psychiatrist, his physician, and the spider with the wailing face: were long gone.

But I'm still here, Jay thought. *And I've got work to do.*

A lot of time was wasted reminiscing about the past. He would have to make up for it now. The documents had to be submitted before eighteen o'clock. Otherwise, a lot of trouble would be awaiting him. Punishment in the government sector could be anything; but it was never pleasant. And that was something he could not afford. He had a life to live. He had mouths to feed.

The faces of his wife and his daughter appeared before his eyes.

His face was sodden with sweat. The eye lenses of his gas mask had turned foggy. He took off the mask, wincing at the pungent, dusty air of the city. He had still not gotten used to it.

Wiping his face and neck with a wet wipe, and throwing the stained cloth in the trashcan, he put on his gas mask again.

He picked up the files from the floor, and pressed the power button of his laptop.

Fuck you, he mouthed at the spider.

Once again, the tap-tap-tapping of fingers on the keyboard joined the city's noisy choir.

You have to face your fears, the old psychiatrist's voice fleeted in the air. ***You can't run away from them.***

16 Arachnid

Chapter 2

When Jay clicked on "Print," it was a quarter past seventeen. As the papers clattered out of the printer, he stretched in his chair, cracking his knuckles. He was drenched in sweat. The spider was still sitting on the same discoloured spot of the flaky wall. It had not moved an inch.

"Hot, isn't it?" Jay said out aloud.

The spider did not answer.

Hands behind his head, Jay looked at the creepy crawler. He fought a repulsive feeling that tried to get over him. Anybody else in his place would have given in to the feeling and squashed the spider by now. Everything around him could be used for that: his shoes, the thick notebooks, and the fat folders spread all over the place. He would just have to pick one up, and *splat*! Finished. The ant army would then do the job of taking the corpse away. But Jay had never, despite his terrible aversion, killed a spider under any circumstance. For instance, once he had seen a spider in the office restroom. It was sitting in the urinal. As usual, it reminded Jay of the incident from his childhood: a "scary" spider had made him piss his pants. Now he had the opportunity to piss on one of its lesser-intimidating kinsmen and avenge his humiliation. But he knew that the trauma would not go away just like that. He also had nothing against that particular spider. It was just a dumb creature waiting to get flushed and drowned down the gutters. Jay used another urinal.

And despite his attempts of spider-proofing his own house, a spider or two would always show up whenever he did some cleaning. He had no idea where they came from. Fighting a mighty urge to squash them under his slippers, he allowed the spiders to crawl on to the dustpan, and holding it as far away from his body as possible, he took them outside, and let them free. *Go wherever you want to. Just stay away from me.*

On one such occasion, a particularly stubborn spider, not paying heed to the nudging broom and dustpan, ultimately leapt upon Jay's shoulder. Fortunately, Sunita was at work, and Ginny was yet to arrive in this world, and so nobody stood witness to the acrobatics Jay performed in the house that day. But that spider's life, too, was spared.

Arranging the printed documents in a folder, Jay slung his office bag over his shoulder. He turned off the table fan. "You're fired," he said.

Taking one last look at the spider on the wall, he walked out of the room.

The air did not feel any different in the corridor. *Even if the A.C. was working, it'd have felt the same*, Jay thought.

That, of course, was only a consolation. One had to say such things to oneself in order to create a sense of contentment, which, although made under false pretenses, did the job of fooling the mind.

It's a hot and uncomfortable room, he said to himself. *With the A.C., it'd have been a cold and uncomfortable room.*

And the gullible mind assented quietly.

The security guard outside the superintendent's chamber scanned Jay with a biotech scanner. These new scanners not only detected metallic objects, but could also check the body temperature, pulse rate, and identity of the scanned person.

It amazed Jay how a machine knew him better than he himself did. And he envied the machine for that.

A flurry of cold wind hit Jay in the face as the door was pushed open.

The superintendent's private chamber was isolated from the rest of the post office. It was like a piece of a jigsaw puzzle forcefully shoved into a space where it did not belong. For a single officer, the room was way too large. In fact, except for the three-foot tall superintendent, everything in the room was oversized: starting from the air conditioner to the waste basket: a luxury befitting a higher official. The room was regularly sanitized, and the air freshened, so that the superintendent did not have to wear a gas mask all the time. Jay had nothing against that.

The superintendent was seated on his heightened chair. Another employee was in the room. Looking at his number tag, Jay recognised the man as Arijit Banerjee.

"It's really difficult to work like this, Sir," he was saying.

"I know, I know," the superintendent said. "Our specialist Bagchi will take care of it."

"Three hours in that room without an A.C.!" Arijit said with a massive sigh, which seemed to last for an entire minute. "I can't work like this," he added.

The superintendent raised his eyebrows and stared at Arijit with his toad-like eyes.

Jay shook his head.

Idiot!

"I-I mean... it's... it's ***difficult*** to work like this," Arijit said, realizing his flub up.

"Bagchi will be here soon," the superintendent said, smiling.

"I ***am*** working, Sir. It's just the heat-"

"I understand, Mr One-one-six. I totally understand. The A.C. will be fixed soon."

"Sure. Sure, Sir. No hurries. Thank you, Sir."

Arijit looked at Jay as he scooted out of the room. Jay could ***feel*** the fear in his eyes through his gas mask.

After Jay handed over the documents, the superintendent cleared his throat, and said, "Mr

Seventy-two, I know your A.C. also needs repairing. Bagchi will fix it soon."

"That's fine, Sir," Jay said. "But I can contact another repairman if that's okay with you."

"Very well," the superintendent said. "I'll call Bagchi and cancel your appointment, then."

'Appointment'? What is this man, a dentist?

"Thank you, Sir."

"Who is this repairman? I'll have to run a quick background check before we let him in. I have complete faith in you as an employee, but it's the protocol. Please don't mind."

"No, no. Of course not. His name is Tapas Sinha. He lives in Workers' Colony-5."

The superintendent typed something on his laptop with his short, thick fingers.

"I don't find his name on the Ministry log," he said.

"He's not working for them. He's self-employed."

The superintendent hesitated for a moment, and then said, "All right. I'll email you his pass."

Thanking him, Jay walked out of the palatial chamber and back into the regular world.

The voice machine was announcing the departing postal officers.

"Signing off: number fifty: Jonathan Austin. Signing off: number twenty-one: Nisha Tamang." It went on.

Nobody exchanged words or greetings. Dragging their feet, the postal workers were walking out of the office.

P-one, the cleaning man, was brooming the linoleum floor.

Jay walked up to him.

"Get my room cleaned, P-one, will you?"

"Sir. Certainly, Sir."

"There's a... um... a spider in there. Get it out."

"A spider, Sir? Did it jump on you, Sir, by any chance, Sir?"

Jay raised his eyebrows.

"Did it *jump* on me? No. No, it didn't."

"My grandmother used to say, Sir, if a spider gets up on your clothes, Sir, you receive new clothes, Sir."

That one time when a spider had jumped on Jay, did he get new clothes?

Nope.

"Okay," he said. "Just get it out of there."

"Yes, Sir."

"Bye."

"Signing off: number seventy-two: Jayaraj Mukherjee," the voice machine chimed as Jay walked out of the City-8 Post Office.

The last light of the day shaded the city with a pale hue of sepia. It would soon get cold. Airships were hovering in the orange sky, the advertisements on their bodies blurred by the yellow haze that had cloaked the entire world. The roads were crowded with commuting automobiles; the pavements were crowded with commuting men and women. The hookers were already out on the streets holding placards containing information about their body types and the special services they offered. They never wore gas masks so that their clients could see their faces. The only other people who did not wear gas masks were the working class people. They had somehow gotten used to the city. And Jay lauded them for that, because he knew he could never do so.

He *hated* the city.

Fortunately, his house was at Maxwell Corner, a suburb located away from the city's constant clamour.

It was difficult to get a patch of land those days (but not impossible, as it had now become). There were not enough vacant spaces for building new houses. Every single inch of the city was already crowded with buildings of all shapes and sizes. For erecting new buildings in the heart of the city, pre-existing buildings had to be demolished. This resulted in drawn-out legal battles, whose outcomes were almost always welcomed with more legal battles.

Despite this, people preferred living in the heart of the metropolis as it was more efficient to be within the vicinity of all kinds of commodities that City-8 had to offer. But Jay did not want to wear a gas mask while sitting inside his own house. And so, he and Sunita spent almost all their savings in buying a piece of land at Maxwell Corner, where they built a house they could address as their "home".

Once the doors of their house were closed, the city's noises were considerably reduced. However, there was an omnipresent sound that had become a part of the city. Decades ago, this sound was considered noise. But with time, people learned to live with it. Meteorologists called this "The Song of the City," but the old folk, who had heard better sounds during their days, called it "The Screaming Ghosts of the Past." Jay did not like either of those nomenclatures.

As he strolled towards the bus stop, he felt a hand on his shoulder.

Turning around, he saw four men in the post office uniform. Jay recognized them by their number tags: Chuck Reang (70), Suresh Sharma (85), Kaushik Sanyal (121), and Faiz Ali (63).

In a world where friendship, as it was once known, did not exist, these four men and Jay were close to being what could be categorized as "friends." Jay, however, was not very fond of them. In fact, he was not fond of any of his colleagues or superiors. He disliked the haughty air that surrounded them, and he never felt like being a part of their frivolous conversations. But he had been working with these men for over a decade now. Therefore, the bonding, although superficial, was inevitable. If there was anybody Jay could genuinely call a "friend" (besides Sunita), was his neighbour Soumik. That was more than enough, because in this world, there was no place for friends anymore. There was no time for them.

"There's good news," Chuck said.

"Really?" Jay said.

"Our man's getting married," Faiz said, patting Kaushik on the back.

"Woah! Congratulations!"

He shook Kaushik's hand.

"So, who's the lucky girl?"

"Her name is Priya," Kaushik said. "We met on MeetUp."

"MeetUp? The dating site?"

"Yeah. One of my relatives knows an employee there. He got me a discount coupon for a premium profile. And-"

"And you got 'em benefits for real!" Suresh said, laughing aloud.

"I sure did!"

"Like a spider," Chuck said.

"What?" Jay yawped.

"Yeah. See, the web... is like the cobweb... get it? And the people there, sitting and waiting for something to get trapped in it, are like spiders."

"So, who's the spider here, and who's the prey?" Faiz asked.

"I guess only time will tell," Kaushik said.

"And what if both of you are spiders?"

"Then I guess our Kaushik will be eaten," Suresh said, and the men burst out laughing. All except Jay. He was still trying to process the words that were getting exchanged in this conversation.

"Okay, boys," Chuck said. "Rest of it in the club. Jay, you're coming with us."

"The... the club?" Jay said.

"Our *Wild East*!"

Shit!

Every ten days, Jay's "friends" followed the ritual of having some drinks at the Wild East Club at Queens Road. For several years, Jay was also a pilgrim of this pilgrimage, but he had been on the wagon for over three years now.

The discontinuation had coincided with the birth of his daughter, so his colleagues assumed that it was for her that he had stopped drinking.

But that was just a coincidence.

Jay had his reasons.

They remained seated deep in the crevices of Jay's mind, along with all his other secrets. Secrets that could never come out, like the fact that he was once an arachnophobe.

(*We all have our secrets.*)

"Oh c'mon!" Chuck said. "It's Kaushik's bachelor party. I don't think your wife will mind."

"No, no. It's not that. My car is in the hospital. It broke down five days ago. I've been using the bus to-"

"Don't worry about that. We'll take my car. There's plenty of room there for all of us."

Sometimes it becomes impossible to refuse an invitation. This was one such occasion.

But that club...

Jay had decided to never step foot in there again.

"I'll just go get the car," Chuck said, and walked towards the post office's parking lot.

Stick with the guys, and don't drink too much. That's all.

Right?

"What the hell!" Suresh suddenly cried out, looking at his phone.

"What happened?"

"Arijit Banerjee got sacked!"

"*What?*"

"Misdemeanour."

Jay sighed. He knew it would happen.

"Misdemeanour? He seemed like a nice chap!" Kaushik said.

"I wonder what happened."

"The A.C. in his room was not working," Jay said. "And he said he couldn't work like that."

"Said to whom?"

"The superintendent."

"How do you know about this?"

"I was there when it happened."

The men looked at one another. Suresh slapped his gas-masked forehead. "Well, he had it comin', then."

Jay did not know how to respond to that. But he did not have to think much, as Chuck's shiny red car pulled in before them.

Suresh informed Chuck about the dismissal of Arijit Banerjee. He made two clicking sounds with his tongue and said, "Too bad."

Getting inside the car, Jay realised how long it had been since he had socialised with this group. Ever since he had stopped accompanying them to the Wild East Club, his only interactions with them were limited to the obligatory exchange of pleasantries in the hallways. Now he felt like an alien in their midst.

The car door closed with a thud, and along with that sound, Jay's train of thoughts fell right off its tracks.

On the upper right corner of the car's windscreen, there was an ornate cobweb.

Jay had seen all kinds of stickers on windshields: owners' names, designations, random Chinese letters, and even those of cracked glass. But a spider's web?

This is ridiculous. That's way too many spider references for one day.

Taking his eyes off the web, Jay took out his phone. He had to inform Sunita about the sudden plan.

"I'll be late tonight," he typed a text message. "Kaushik's bachelor party. Don't stay up." He read the message thrice and then added, "Love you."

(*I promise it won't happen again.*)

Pressing the "Send" button, he looked up at the sticker on the windshield, as the car made its way to Queens Road.

(***Never again.***)

Chapter 3

As always, the road was crowded with automobiles. Stuck on a red light, Jay's colleagues were having a raucous discussion about the government's new policy of privatising water. Jay only nodded his head occasionally, and kept his responses limited to "yes" and "hmm." He did have his own opinions on the matter, but judging by the intensity of the conversation, and the ecstatic tirades of his colleagues, he decided to zip his lips.

"Look at that hick," Suresh suddenly said, pointing at the window.

A man wearing nothing but a pair of ragged trousers was standing on the pavement. Arms crossed around his body, he was constantly turning his head from one side to the other, as if he were looking for someone. He cringed at the men in suits and the women in dresses who walked past him.

"Doesn't even have a shirt on!" Suresh grimaced.

"Maybe he doesn't have any," Chuck said.

"Doesn't have clothes? Who doesn't have fuckin' clothes?"

"He looks kinda scared though, doesn't he?" Jay said.

Faiz shook his head. "This is the third time this month I'm seeing a sight like this. They're increasing in number. Goodness knows where they come from."

"Or where they go," Chuck added.

"But who are 'they'?"

"Maybe working class men?"

"They don't walk around naked. Even *they* have some dignity."

"Why doesn't the Federation do something about them?" Suresh said.

"They have better things to worry about."

"Hmm." Jay nodded, looking at the shirtless man. He was still searching for someone. Or something. But how would he see anything through the blackened windows of the cars? How would he see the faces behind the masks?

The traffic lights turned green, and Chuck's car slowly started moving forward. The shirtless man stared at the car as it drove past him. Suddenly, he locked eyes with Jay.

His eyes widened, and he opened his mouth. But before Jay could even realise what was going on, the car picked up its speed, and the man was devoured by the rushing city. All this happened in a split-second. But to Jay, it seemed like an eternity had passed as their eyes had met. Nothing, however, was exchanged in those moments of eternity.

Those eyes were trying to convey a message. But what could it be?

That's just stupid. Jay shook his head.

There was no way the man could have seen him through the blackened windows of the car. And even if he could, he would have only seen Jay's gas mask. He also could not have recognized him by his number tag, since his jacket was covering his post office uniform.

Stupid.

Dusting the thoughts away, he brought his mind back inside the car.

The men were still debating on the proposed Water Bill.

"... isn't it?" Faiz was blabbering.

"Hmm," Jay said, nodding his head.

Stupid.

Chapter 4

It was already dark when they reached the clubhouse.

"Wow!" Jay said, stepping out of the car.

Everything there, except the name of the clubhouse, had changed.

Everything looked new. Grand.

The Wild East Club was now a three-storey building: the highest allowed for a middle class clubhouse. A pink neon sign screamed its incompatible name with bright blinking lights and fancy fonts. Electric lanterns hung from the eaves.

The open parking lot beside the clubhouse was replaced by a multi-storey car park. It was connected to the clubhouse on the left, and to a new four-storey building on the right. The car park was taller than both the buildings.

In front of the four-storey building was a wrought-iron gate, over which, in a semicircle, were the words "Queens Road Nursery School."

Nice place for a school, Jay thought.

"They've shifted the strip club to the second floor," Chuck informed Jay as they walked towards the clubhouse entrance.

"And you've gotta check out the chicks," Suresh said, rubbing his palms together. "Really, *really* great stuff. Gave an old man a heart attack the other day."

"What?" Jay said.

"For real. He was getting a nude lap dance. Had a heart attack. Died right there."

"You're kidding!"

"No, no. It really happened," Kaushik said. "They didn't even realise the guy was dead, and the show went on."

"They literally humped a dead body for over an hour," Faiz said.

"Oh, I'd like to die like that," Suresh said.

"Yeah, you'll die anyway if your wife hears this," Faiz said, and the men burst out laughing. All but Jay.

"And... what's on the top floor?" he asked.

"The VIP lounge," Chuck answered. "FKA the Red Room."

On hearing that name, a spider scurried somewhere inside Jay's head.

(stomp on it stomp on it stomp-)

"Hey! Check this out!" a male voice suddenly yelled out from behind.

"Street show!" yelled another one.

Jay, snapping out of his musings, turned around. A small crowd of applauding people had gathered near the car park.

A man in a denim jacket was lying on the ground, sticking his arms on to the sides of his body and bringing his legs together, forming a straight line. His eyes were rolled up, his tongue stuck out of his mouth, and he made abrupt movements, shaking his entire body without loosening his limbs. He flopped on the ground like a fish taken out of water. Coins and bills were scattered all around him.

"That's weird," Kaushik said.

"He got moves though," Suresh said.

"Does he perform here every day?" Jay asked.

"It's the first time I've seen him here," Chuck answered.

Is this some sort of a dance? Jay wondered. *A mime? What is this supposed to mean?*

Chuck tossed a coin before the man. It ricocheted off the ground and hit him on the face. But the man, without even a flinch, continued with his routine.

Jay reached into his pocket, but Chuck stopped him.

"That'll be enough," he said. "Let's go in now."

Leaving the performer and the cheering crowd behind, the men walked towards the clubhouse.

Two bouncers, wearing helmet-like masks, were standing on either side of the entrance door. Their silver corduroy suits sparkled brightly, as if small bulbs were embedded onto the fabric. Their name tags read "Rick" and "Atif."

Jay knew Rick and Atif were the clubhouse bouncers, but he had never seen their faces. Who knew if they were the **same** Rick and Atif?

Was it not possible that just like the clubhouse, its bouncers were also renovated, with their names unchanged?

Who can tell what's under the mask?

Although Jay's colleagues visited the place every six days, the security protocol was strictly maintained. The men stood in a queue as the bouncers checked their identity cards, and scanned them with biotech scanners.

Reaching the front of the line, Jay got a closer look at the bouncers. They wore the same clothes as they used to wear three years ago. They were built the same way: standing over seven-foot tall, with shoulders so wide that one man was enough to block the entrance door, and biceps that popped out of their sleeves.

But were they the same people?

"Good evening, Mr Mukherjee!" the man with the "Atif" name tag said. "Long time no see!"

An unknown voice?

Jay opened his mouth without knowing what to say, when someone screamed from behind.

The sound had come from the crowd around the street performer.

"Please! Please, help!" a woman's voice was screaming.

Jay hurried towards the crowd, which had turned bigger.

The performer was still doing his shtick, flopping on the ground. A woman in a blue sari was kneeling beside him.

"Help!" she yelled, looking at the spectators. "Please, please call a doctor!"

The crowd cheered.

"Realistic," Chuck said.

"You see, serious talent doesn't get appreciated nowadays." Faiz said, clapping. "These people deserve a better audience."

"Animals!" the woman shrieked. She tried to get the man up, but he kept trembling on the ground uncontrollably.

The crowd cheered and applauded louder.

"I think something's wrong," Jay said.

"*I* think it's brilliant," Chuck said.

"Let me through! Let me see!" a thunderous voice bellowed from the crowd. "I'm a doctor!"

A short man, no more than three feet in height, pushed through the crowd, dragging a huge briefcase that was almost his own size. He wore a fluorescent violet suit, and oversized sports shoes that made his feet look comically large.

The crowd roared with laughter. Jay's colleagues joined them.

Squatting near the flopping man's head, the little man said in his thunderous voice, "He's having an epileptic fit!"

"Let's go," Chuck said, tugging at Jay's arm. "This'll go on for a while."

"We don't have a phone," the woman in the blue sari was saying as Chuck pulled Jay away from the spectacle.

"They seem like professionals," Kaushik said.

Jay's head was buzzing as the men went through another round of biotech scanning, and then the clubhouse door swung open with a beep. The sound of bass-boosted disco beats drifted out into the murky city air, creating a mix-tape with the song of the city. It was the same disco music they played here three years ago. That was the *only* music ever played in the Wild East Club.

Taking one last look at the street performers, who were still carrying on with their act, Jay walked into the clubhouse.

(*Don't look back.*)

He stepped into another world

(*Don't look*)

as the door closed behind him.

(*Don't*)

Chapter 5

It was half past one o'clock in the morning when Jay returned home.

There was a time when one o'clock instantly conjured images of a sleeping world: deserted roads, stray dogs, houses covered in darkness, and unknown dangers. But those images, along with the time, were long gone. The metropolis did not sleep anymore. Its streets were never deserted; synthetic dogs that required neither food nor affection roamed around; there was never a moment of darkness due to the dazzling city lights. Only the unknown dangers were left behind, lurking in the lights, in every nook and corner of the city, feigning various figures and frames.

Jay closed the door as quietly as possible. With a soft click, the volume of the city's noises was turned down. Tossing away his gas mask, he breathed in the domestic air of the air-conditioned room.

Home.

Although he was not drunk, his head was aching, and the awkwardly looped disco music was still ringing in his ears. The red and blue fluorescent lights of the club flashed before his eyes as he stood in the dark drawing room. A glass with a red smudge near its rim appeared before him, but he rubbed his eyes and shook his head, getting rid of the image.

The fuck's wrong with me!

He had only had one glass of champagne. His colleagues, however, got completely wasted.

Kaushik, despite Jay's implorations, went into the VIP lounge.

"It's his last party as a bachelor," Faiz said. "Let the man enjoy it!"

Suresh got his coveted lap dance from a topless stripper, and Faiz danced his guts out – he twisted and jumped and shimmied until he threw up. Chuck got so drunk that he had to leave his car at the car park, and Jay had to get back home on a public bus.

He knew Sunita would not be mad at him for coming home at this hour. He had been this late only on one other occasion before. And that was well over three years ago - the last time he had gone to the club.

(*the last time...*)

The light in the hallway was kept on.

It shone its dim red light on the corridor that led to the bedroom.

Red? But wasn't it yellow?

Jay was not feeling drunk at all. It was impossible for one glass of champagne to get him so drunk so that he would start seeing one colour in place of another.

Standing below the little bulb, he looked up. If he were really drunk, even this twelve-watt light bulb would have pricked his temples. But it did not.

Maybe it* is *red, he thought, and tiptoed towards the bedroom.

He stopped in front of a custom-designed door on the left side of the hallway. Cracking the door open, he peeked inside. Little Ginny, hugging her big teddy, was fast asleep in her little bed.

Seeing her silhouette, Jay felt a desperate love for his daughter. He wanted to hold her in his arms; he wanted to hear her voice. He knew that it was only a matter of time before she would unknowingly start drifting away from him. Right now, she was dependent on him because she was weak. She was only a child. The confusing, unrecognizable feelings of vulnerability and fear inside her made her stick to her father. Once she would recognize her attachment as a consequence of her vulnerability, she would let go of him. That was inevitable. She would then want to be independent, and her father would become an obstacle in her way. And very soon, he would lose her. He would lose a part of himself.

Sighing, he tore his eyes away from her, and made for his bedroom.

The bedroom door was left ajar. He stepped inside.

The room was basking in the pallid blue and yellow city lights, which, entering through the closed window panes, had crept into bed with Jay's wife. Jay would have preferred seeing Sunita bathe in the splendorous white moonlight, but that was impossible. The moon was blocked with all the looming towers and the stone monuments and the massive zeppelins. A few parks had been opened on the western part of the city, away from the busy streets, where couples could go moon watching. But it went out of fashion very soon with the introduction of the television show *Moonwatch*: a series based on moon watching. The show had no story, no plot, and no characters. The episodes were just twenty-minute video footage of the moon recorded the previous night. In case of a new moon, there would just be a black screen.

There was no longer the need to look at the sky or go outside when people could sit at home and watch the moon on their television screens and mobile phones. Consequently, the show became a massive hit, and went on to win several prestigious awards.

All this seemed madness to Jay. But his opinion did not matter. He was only a middle class man working for the Federation at a post office.

Sunita's long, black hair was concealing her sleeping face. Although Jay was not sure of how he himself looked like, he could recall Sunita's facial features with vivid detail. And confidence. Her large brown eyes that could see through Jay's soul, her angular eyebrows that danced as she spoke, her full lips that tasted of cherries – he remembered everything.

But I can't remember my own face.

He also remembered the first time he had seen her, back when they were studying at the university. That was fourteen years ago. Jay could not recall the exact day, or the moment he had fallen in love with her, but he knew, without a doubt, that it must have been a beautiful feeling. ***Probably was.*** They stuck together throughout their course at the university, and always supported each other academically, and emotionally. Both of them had graduated with good marks and moral points which made them eligible for taking the Normal Functionality Test. They passed the test with scores good enough to get them government jobs. Jay was placed into the postal department, whereas Sunita was hired by the auditing department. Two months later, they moved into a small, two-room apartment in the heart of the city. After a year, with the approval of their parents, the couple signed a marriage contract at their local marriage bureau. Having saved enough money, and after inheriting a fair sum after his parents' death four years later, Jay and Sunita bought a piece of vacant land at Maxwell Corner, where they built their house – a house worthy of admiration. Ginny was born the following year.

Except for Ginny's birth, nothing significant or special happened in Jay and Sunita's married life. Every married couple (who also happened to be government employees) apparently lived a similar lifestyle. That way of living was lauded and heavily promoted by the

Federation. They believed it was due to their efforts that there had been a significant drop in the divorce rates of the country.

"The key to it is to reduce all kinds of communication," the Nobel Laureate Dr Park In Son had said in an interview. "Lesser communication between two people would mean lesser chances of misunderstandings, and subsequently, lesser chances of having a breakup. We must aim for the total stoppage of communication with our partners. Effective communication is something that must only be applied in workplaces, and not in romantic relationships."

Jay did not question the practicality of that statement because the government doctors were always right. They always had the facts and figures to support their claims and statements.

And in his case, he could look at his own marriage as an example.

I remember all that, he thought. *But I don't remember my own face.*

Looking at Sunita's hidden face, he wondered, "What if I moved her hair and a different face looked back at me? Would I be scared? Surprised?"

This strange contemplation was the outcome of a peculiar question that Sunita had asked him earlier that day when they had sat down for breakfast. Breakfast and dinner were the only occasions when the Mukherjee family got the chance to spend some time together. The conversations in the morning, although monotonous, were always more affable than the ones that took place at night. There was nothing unusual, nothing new. Thus, Jay was taken aback by the abrupt question Sunita had dropped on him.

"If I become somebody else," she had asked, "will you still love me?"

Jay stopped stirring his spoon in his bowl of cereal. He did not look up at her. He stared at the spoon in his hand, wondering why it had stopped.

"It's gonna get hot and humid today," the weatherman was saying on the television. "No, I'm not talking about my girlfriend here." A prolonged laughter track followed the line. "See you tonight, baby!" More laughs.

Fucking laughter tracks!

"Jay?" Sunita said.

"Huh?"

"Look at me."

Stuffing a spoonful of cereal in his mouth, he looked up at her.

"If I become somebody else," she paused here for a moment, and then continued slowly, "will you still love me?"

Jay realised that he had stuffed way too much cereal inside his mouth. He gulped it down with some milk.

(*Answer her. It's just a question.*)

Wiping his mouth with a napkin, he said, "What do you mean, 'become somebody else'?"

"You know, like... become a different person."

"Different how? Physically, or mentally?"

"Does that matter?"

"Uh-huh. You could change in appearance and still have the same mental... psychological build. That would be a physical change. On the other hand, your psychological state might change, giving you a new identity, while your, uh, physical state might remain the same. That's a mental or psychological change."

What the fuck am I talking about?

Sunita thought about it for a few seconds, and then said, "Either way."

"Of course." Jay shrugged. "Of course, I'll still love you."

Sunita was about to say something, when Ginny cried out, "And what about me? What about me?"

"How can I ever stop loving my princess?" Jay said, holding her hand.

"Really, papa?"

"Yes." He looked at Sunita, and smiled.

(*Just a question.*)

Sunita stirred in bed. "You're here?" her sleepy voice said.

"Sorry, I'm so late."

"No, no," she said.

Jay held his breath as she turned towards him. She brushed her hair away from her face, and

(**who-**)

Jay exhaled with ease.

Yes. It was Sunita. Her name was Sunita. The way he remembered her.

"It's okay," she said. "Why shouldn't you have fun?"

Yeah. Some fun.

He smiled.

"Come here," she said, extending her arms.

Jay walked towards her, his body anticipating the thrill of touching her skin – the skin he loved so dearly – the skin of his wife.

She wrapped her arms around Jay's neck, and they shared a kiss. Her delicate tongue felt warm in his mouth.

"Did they get the A.C. fixed?" she asked, lying down.

"No. I'm gonna ask Tapas to fix it."

"Okay."

"How was work?" Jay asked, undressing. His clothes reeked of sweat and smoke and alcohol and the city.

"Boring, as always," she said. "You know, I was thinking... We are working too much. We should go on a holiday."

Holiday. Jay mulled over the word. When was the last time he got a holiday? Back in school? It was incredible to think of all the holidays and vacations they used to enjoy back then. During his time in middle school, there used to be a long summer vacation, a short spring vacation, and another long winter vacation. Craziest of all, there was one entire day of holiday every seven days! It was called "Sunday."

Or am I imagining it?

The days were grouped into seven days, called "weeks," and all the days of the week had names assigned to them. Monday, Tuesday, Wednesday, Thursday, Friday, Saturday, and Sunday. *How can I remember all that, but not remember my fucking face?* That system was discarded eighteen years ago, and was replaced by the more efficient "Day-Number" system, which listed the days as Day-1, Day-2, Day-3... all the way to Day-365, with an additional Day-0 on leap years. And instead of twelve months, a year was divided into five months (named after the five World Leaders), each month consisting of seventy-three days. When Jay was in high school, all kinds of holidays, except the Sundays, were discarded. By the time he got into college, the new calendar was universally accepted, and Sundays were retired.

Vacations and holidays were a thing of the past. The government institutions did not authorize any kind of break. Taking a holiday would mean taking a casual leave without pay. But Jay and Sunita had earned and saved enough to be able to afford a short vacation.

"Yeah," Jay said. "Yeah, I suppose we could."

"We'll talk about it tomorrow."

"Yeah, um..." Jay hesitated for a moment. "What's with that light out there?"

"What light?"

"The red bulb in the hallway."

"You put it there seven days ago."

"I did?" Jay scratched his head.

"Yeah, I was surprised that you fixed a red light there."

"I did? Hmm..." When did he change the light? And why on earth did he put a red one?

"See?" Sunita said, sitting up. "You are stressed out. You are forgetting things."

"Forgetting things, huh?" Jay muttered. He racked his brain. But the memory of the light bulb had been completely erased from his mind.

Sunita pressed his hand. Had all these years of living together created a special sort of understanding between them? Was that even possible?

No. They were two separate individuals with distinct personalities, living their disparate lives. They were like two parallel lines running so close to one another that they caused an illusion that they would, at some point, intersect. Bound by marriage and love, they were close – so close that it seemed like they would join and become one. But they never did. And they never could.

And there was nothing wrong with that.

That was normal. That was how it was supposed to be.

"Go back to sleep," Jay said. "I'll take a shower."

"Use hot water," Sunita said, and lay back in bed, covering her face with the grey (**red?**) sheet.

Jay turned on the bathroom lights, and walked in.

Before looking into the bathroom mirror, he closed his eyes and tried to remember what he looked like. He hardly got the chance to look at his own face, be it in the mirror, or in photographs. And so whenever he looked into the mirror, an uncanny face looked back at him.

He thought about the general facial features of humans, running his hand over his face as if to ensure that they were present.

Eyes. Ears. Nose. Lips.

Yes. They were present. But he did not know what kind of an appearance they created collectively.

I don't know who I am?

Taking a deep breath, he opened his eyes.

(*You have to face your fears.*)

The mirror was too hazy to form a clear image. And the central portion of the mirror, which would have otherwise revealed his face, was covered by something.

Something that made him shudder and recoil.

A spider.

How did it get in here?

Luckily, this spider did not have anything drawn on its back. It was another one of those brown, tiny house spiders.

A mop was leaning against the corner of the bathroom. But what if the spider jumped on him? Would he react the same way he had done all those years ago? Could he risk revealing his secret?

One had to be particularly careful while dealing with secrets. Jay believed that the only way to keep a secret safe was to become unaware of it. That was the reason he locked up all his secrets in a vault, bound it with a chain, and kept it in a recluse corner of his mind. He was always cautious about treading there. He tried his best to stay away from that place. However, throughout the day, one incident after another had been tugging at the chain. That was dangerous. If one secret found its way out, the rest would definitely follow suit.

And that would have some pretty serious repercussions, as there were way too many secrets settled in Jay's vault.

"I'll take care of you in the morning," Jay whispered to the spider. "But you'll probably just disappear by then, right?"

The spider answered with silence.

"Well then, I'll find you out." Jay said.

He turned on the shower. The cold water droplets stabbed him like sharp needles. The water trickled down his body, turning brown as it reached the floor. Swirling about the drain, the muddy water disappeared into it forever.

Jay looked at the mirror. All he could see was a smear of colours

Is this what I look like?

and the spider.

A creature he despised so much.

Getting out of the shower, he towelled himself dry. But his legs were still wet. He kept wiping them frantically, but the wet feeling was not going away.

(*Stop*)

He knew it would not dry like that, but he kept rubbing his legs

(*Stop!*)

until the towel scraped his skin.

I'm losing it.

"Screw you," he mouthed at the spider,

(and the mirror) and hastened out of the bathroom.

He grabbed a t-shirt.

What colour is it? Black? Blue? Red? Yellow? Fuck it.

Tossing the t-shirt aside, he got into bed. Sunita snuggled close to him.

Jay felt her warm body. Her soft skin. He felt her shape and curves through her cotton t-shirt.

He recapitulated the day's happenings. They did not seem to make any sense. Something was very wrong. Throughout the day, he had met with one shock after another. A series of coincidences, all on the same day? What were the odds?

It was also very strange that he remembered certain events that had taken place several years ago, but could not remember something he had done seven days ago? *Seven days. A week.* He remembered a bunch of useless information from his childhood; he could also recall all the names of the week; but he forgot about the light bulb. How? But then again, he could not even remember his own face.

Was he overworking himself? Crammed into a little room, surrounded by contraptions, breathing through a respirator, and dreading the deadlines – was all this taking a toll on him? What if the documents he had submitted earlier that day reflected his physical and mental exhaustion? What would the Federation do? Punish him? Punish him for being a victim of the same system that the Federation itself had designed? Was that system really as efficient as the Federation claimed it to be?

Were they not turning the people into machines?

But would they risk doing that after what had happened with the androids?

Four years ago, the World A.I. Project failed after an android named Reficul rallied the androids to take up arms against the humans. They had planned for a coup, but as soon as the symptoms of rebellion were noticed in them, they were all shut down, and their bodies were disposed of. It was rumoured that Reficul and a few of his followers escaped the police, and went into hiding, forming the "Underground Army" – the government's only opposition. The Federation, however, claimed that the Underground Army consisted of nothing more than five high school dropouts who wanted to disrupt the peace of the country, and that Reficul's body was on display at the International Scientific Research Institution. But the relief was short-lived. Reficul, along with his followers, showed up during an address by the Vice President, killed all his guards, beheaded him on live television, and wrote "JOIN US" on the walls with his blood.

The Federation released a statement an hour later, calling the incident an "elaborate prank just for the lulz." The Vice President appeared live on television the very next day, having a good laugh about it.

But Jay did not buy it. He could not even tell who he was watching on TV, as the Vice President always wore a gas mask. Nobody had ever seen his face. And nobody knew his name.

What surprised Jay the most was how the people had not seen this coming. The creations turned on their creators when they realised that the latter possessed nothing to exercise their feigned superiority over the former. Human beings, several decades ago, had not only renounced creationism, but had also renounced God – the concept of God – the concept of a superior being who was responsible for their existence. Mankind did not want to be slaves to an abstract concept. Then how did they expect the androids – conscious beings far more advanced than their creators – to accept them as their superiors, and work as their slaves?

Only the creatures with free will could do something so erratic as to refuse the supremacy of their creators. And so, the production of synthetic men and women was stopped. But plants, animals, and birds continued to be manufactured in the factories.

Since they couldn't turn the machines into servile people, they're turning the servile people into machines?

If that was the case, then who would save them?

Decades ago, people had God to turn to. They had faith. Now, there was nothing.

Nothing?

Jay felt his wife's warm breath on his shoulder. He thought about his daughter sleeping in the adjoining room.

Nothing.

He pondered over the question Sunita had asked him earlier in the morning.

(If I become somebody else, will you still love me?)

What if I turned into somebody else? Would she still love me?

Jay imagined waking up the next morning with a new face and a new body, preferably younger and healthier. Sunita would be terrified for sure, but Jay would somehow convince her that he was the same old Jayaraj, her husband, the father of her child. Sunita would have no choice but to force herself into accepting the change. And then, she would like it.

Convincing Ginny would be child's play.

"Papa got a new face, darling," they would tell her.

But could he convince himself? Could he get used to the new face and remember it?

The rest of the world would never know, since he would be wearing his gas mask outside. In his office, he would still be Postal Employee Number Seventy-Two. His colleagues would exchange pleasantries with him, and walk right by, without noticing that a new man had taken his place. But what about the biotech scanners? What would they scan? The mind would be Jay's, but the body would be unidentifiable. Were they programmed for adjusting to such a change?

Probably not.

But the humans were. They had been adjusting to various kinds of changes for millions of years now.

Adjusting. Adapting. Enduring. Accepting.

(*Accepting.*)

Yes. It is indeed possible to be in love with someone even if they transform into someone completely different.

But can the transformed ones love themselves?

The question reverberated in Jay's head, mingling with his tinnitus. It slowly mixed with the droning city, and transitioned into the sounds of crashing waves.

Wherever he looked, there was only water. A boundless ocean. It had consumed the entire earth. Everyone was gone, except for Jay. He was standing in the middle of the ocean, smelling the waves and the breeze. They smelled like dust and exhaust smoke and medicines.

Aditya Modak

.

Chapter 6

Feeling a series of persistent jolts, Jay opened his eyes. In the split second of slumber between sleep and wakefulness, he thought there was an earthquake. He tried to get up, but he could not move.

His limbs were spread apart. They were either tied up, or glued to the bed. No. Not the bed. It did not feel like his bed. He could not tell where he was. He had either gone blind, or he was in a place devoured by darkness.

It was impossible to be in complete darkness, even with the eyes closed. With all the bright lights illuminating every inch of the city, and the perpetually burning industrial fires covering the skies, there was never a moment of such obsidian darkness. A tinge of light would always be there. Never having experienced such a blackout before, his eyes ached.

It was a pain induced by darkness.

Where are the lights? Who turned out the lights?

He tried moving his arms and legs again, but they did not budge. It seemed like they were stuck to the unknown trembling surface with superglue.

It was then that Jay realised he could not hear anything. No honking automobiles, no recorded announcements, no whirring helicopters – nothing. The droning city had quietened down. Shut down. The Song of the Earth was not being sung anymore. The Screaming Ghosts of the Past had stopped screaming. Even his tinnitus was cured.

Or did he become deaf?

No. There it was. A sound. A steady thumping sound.

(*Thump. Thump. Thump.*)

The sound of his own heart.

But other than that, there was nothing.

Both the lights and the sounds of the world were turned off.

But how? Why?

The jolts were too faint to be felt substantially, but Jay's senses had somehow become sharper in the dark. He could see the darkness, hear the silence, smell and taste the scentless, insipid air, and feel the faint vibrations of the surface beneath him.

Was he abducted by the Underground Army? Or was he picked up by the Federation?

There had been hushed rumours of awful experiments being carried out by both the Federation and the Underground Army, each faction having its own sets of goals and ambitions. The rumours were the results of several disappearances that had taken place all over the country, and two unexplainable incidents – all of which had occurred within the span of one year. On one occasion, a working class woman, who had gone missing from work, reappeared after one hundred and ninety-one days with an extra pair of arms. She was tactically erased by the police as soon as she was seen on the streets. The Federation later issued a statement calling the woman a dummy designed for a police drill, and that "it" had somehow escaped from the training centre. A young man, however, claimed that the woman was his mother, who had gone missing half a year ago, but his claims were discarded as a stunt for getting cheap publicity. On another occasion, a headless man was seen walking the streets, carrying his head in his hands, asking the pedestrians to help him screw it to his body. When the police tried to tactically erase him, he exploded, killing the policemen and several innocent bystanders. The Federation called it "an unfortunate accident," but the surviving people who had witnessed the incident swore that the headless man had an "X" smeared on his body – the symbol of the Underground Army.

It was possible that either one of the factions had chosen Jay for their experiments.

For the Federation, he would be an easy pick – a conspicuous, insignificant middle class man, who was also working for them. In case things went wrong, the job of erasing him would be much easier. As for the Underground Army, converting a government employee into an android (if they were indeed capable of doing so) would be an easy way to infiltrate into the Federation's system.

Either way, Jay was in a precarious position.

(*fucked*)

And he was being watched.

Even in the utter darkness, he could not shake off the feeling of several eyes watching him. Observing him.

Where am I?

As soon as the question sprang up in his mind, there appeared a sudden flash of light, resembling a dazzling lightning strike.

Piercing through the darkness, it struck him in the eyes.

Behind his shut eyelids, he felt the bright light. He waited for the sounds to return, but they did not.

Very slowly, he opened his eyes.

(*red.*)

A large, red spherical bulb was hovering in the air, a few metres away from him.

There was no ceiling above, there were no walls around. The place looked like an expanse of nothingness, partially lit with the red light, and circumfused by the same impenetrable darkness that had previously occupied it in its entirety.

Jay found himself lying on a hammock hanging over a bottomless pit. It was dark, deep, and ominous. No light reached there. No light could ever reach there. Looking into the abysmal void gave him the jitters. It looked like a wide-open mouth, waiting to consume whatever would fall into it. He grabbed the ropes of the hammock tightly. Stretching across the space, the ropes disappeared into the darkness.

He was bound to the hammock by ropes spun around his wrists and ankles. He noticed that there were far too many ropes for a single hammock, and they were all arranged in a pattern. Shorter, arched pieces of ropes crisscrossed against the longer, radial ones, forming an intricate meshwork.

Jay's heart leapt and crashed against his chest wall. It thudded hard, as if wanting to get out. He realised that-

It's no hammock.

(Thump. Thump. Thump.)

It's a website.

(thump thump thump thump)

He was stuck on a spider's web.

And the vibrations were not the sole effect of Jay's quivering body. Something else was causing the tremors. Something was moving on the other side.

Getting closer.

The vibrations were steadier on the right side. Jay did not want to look there. He had an idea of what he would see.

(don't look don't look don't look)

But his curiosity got the better of him. And he turned his head.

An icy chill ran down his spine.

On the extreme end, where the red illumination faded into the pitch-black darkness, eight little bright red lights were hanging several feet above the ground. Jay knew exactly what they were.

He felt something warm and wet on his legs. The dampness spread all over his body, turning him as cold as ice.

He wanted to scream. But when he opened his mouth, only a soft groan came out of it.

His throat was so dry that it hurt when he swallowed. His head spun as if he were put inside a whirlwind.

The eight little lights were getting bigger. Brighter. Closer.

He tried screaming again. This time, he could not even produce a groan.

How is this possible?

Suddenly, a bright, shiny, spherical object appeared above him.

And the web stopped moving.

Jay could not gather the time to be surprised. The glowing sphere had appeared right out of thin air. Just like the red bulb, it remained suspended in the air without any assistance.

After a few moments, the sphere started rotating, scattering spots of red light all over Jay's body.

He understood what it was.

A disco ball. Just like the one in the Wild East Club.

Finally, Jay heard a faint sound other than that of his heartbeat. Music. As its volume gradually increased, he made out the instruments that were being played.

Saxophone. Cello. Cymbals.

Jazz?

That was not the kind of music played at clubs.

What's that music? Is it from a song?

Another faint sound accompanied the jazz music.

Voices! Voices of people talking. Jay looked around, but he did not see anybody.

Except for the eight balls of fire shrouded by darkness.

Jay tried to focus on the voices. It sounded as if hundreds of people were whispering at the same time. There was no pause, and the words, if any, were undecipherable.

Where are they? And what are they saying?

"Jay!"

Amidst the whispers, he heard a distinct voice call out his name.

"Jay!" it called again, this time louder.

A woman's voice.

Where's it coming from?

"Jay!"

With that, the whispering voices broke off, and the jazz music stopped with a scrubbing noise.

The bulb disappeared. But the place somehow retained the red light. The disco ball continued spinning, scattering the unfounded lights all over the place.

"Hello, Jay!" The female voice echoed throughout the place. "Can you see me?"

He looked around. Nothing.

(Except, of course, those eight glowing eyes.)

He tried to speak, but his voice faltered. His throat was completely dried up.

Gathering some saliva under his tongue, he gulped it down, and then managed to croak, "Are you... are you the spider?"

"The what?"

Sounds of laughter filled up the air. Several people were laughing. Jay realized what it was.

A laughter track.

"Here, Jay," the voice said. "I'm right here."

Jay turned to the left.

A woman was standing a few yards away with her back turned towards him. Her long, straight, black hair, like a shawl, was covering her back. She had on a shiny red bandage dress that made her curves appear prominent. Wearing red high heels, she was standing on the empty space between the strands of web.

She was *floating*.

Slowly, she turned around, and faced Jay.

His heart gave a giant leap as thunderous cheers and claps resounded through the place.

Her eyes, her nose, her ears, her lips – all the constituent features of her face – were missing.

The face looked like a blank sheet of paper.

She was holding a glass in her right hand. It was half-filled with liquid. Little bubbles were dancing in it. It was some kind of a drink.

Champagne?

The female voice spoke up again. "Remember me?"

How's she speaking without a mouth?

Telepathy? No. The voice was not inside his head; it was outside. It was reverberating. It was drifting in the air around him.

But who is she? A human? An android?

The woman tilted her head. She was waiting for him to answer.

Jay tried to speak up again, but his throat hurt so much that even breathing was becoming difficult. He was already thirsty, and seeing the drink made him thirstier.

"W-w- water," he squawked.

(Laughter)

"That doesn't answer my question." The woman shook her faceless head.

"I- I can't see."

"You can't see?"

"The face... Your face."

"Is that so?"

The woman ambled towards Jay. ("Oooooh!") She did not fly over, as one might have expected her to, but walked normally like a regular person. It seemed as if an invisible ground had been built beneath her feet. Her high heels click-clacked across that invisible ground.

She stopped a few meters away from Jay. A bright spotlight fell on her.

Jay was momentarily blinded by the sudden glare of the white light. When he opened his eyes again, the woman did not have an empty face anymore. (Claps)

(***Don't look.***)

She had large, brown eyes. Her left eyebrow was arched higher than her right eyebrow. She had a thin, small nose, and her red lips were curved into a smile that created little dimples on her cheeks. Her large, circular earrings, hanging from her ears, almost touched her bare shoulders.

Her face looked vaguely familiar, but Jay could not recall where he had seen her before. He tried associating that face with a memory – any memory, or an incident – anything that was the cause of this nagging feeling inside him. He looked everywhere, until there was only one place left to be checked. But that was a forbidden place. His conscious mind would never allow him to go there. It was too dangerous. It would be an odyssey with no return.

"Well?" the woman said. This time, her lips moved.

Jay shook his head.

Several voices jeered, "Boooooooo!"

For a second, the smile disappeared from the woman's face. But she smiled again, and walked closer to Jay. (Cheers and claps)

She got so close to him that he could smell her perfume. The fragrance was so powerful (**wonderful**) that even in the face of such an unnatural ordeal, he felt euphoric.

The spider, the web, the thirst, and the fear: everything was gone from his mind. The perfume had taken their place.

His olfactory memories were stirred by it. But what memories was he searching for?

Someone... somewhere... something...

The woman crouched over Jay's sprawled body. The drink in her hand was only a few inches away from his mouth. Although he was dying of thirst, all he wanted was more of that perfume.

The face and the perfume together were tugging at the chains in his mind. The chains, in turn, tugged at a lid – a lid that should not be opened.

The woman lowered her face until her lips were a few centimetres away from Jay's lips. He could smell her lipstick now.

"Now?" she whispered.

Jay shut his eyes.

(*don't look don't look don't speak don't*)

I'm trying to remember.

(*Don't.*)

I'm trying.

(*Don't!*)

I-

(A flash of red light. Lips. A glass. A voice whispering, "I want you." A spider.)

Jay opened his eyes. The lady was still there, looking into his eyes.

"No," he said.

(Audible gasps)

The woman raised her eyebrows. "Thirsty?" she asked.

Jay nodded.

She brought the glass close to Jay's lips. The strong smell of alcohol burned through his nostrils. An old, familiar, and somewhat pleasurable burn.

Jay raised his head to touch the rim of the glass with his lips. But the lady moved her hand away.

(Laughter)

Standing up, she took a few steps back. She held up the glass, and released it. Instead of falling down, it remained floating in the air.

"So," she said, "you don't recognize me?"

Very slowly, her right hand reached over to her left shoulder. It rested on the thin strap of her red dress. Her angular eyebrows did a quick, short jump, and her lips curled into a smile.

Her right hand moved down the length of her left arm, pulling the strap along. Her left hand imitated the same movements for the right shoulder strap.

The velvety dress slid off her body.

(Whistles, cheers, and claps.)

It appeared as if the woman had shed off her skin, revealing a new one – an exquisite, malty skin – untouched by the multitudinous worldly sensations.

This "new" skin was fresh – devoid of all the materialism that ruled the world – the bare, naked skin.

Stepping out of her discarded skin-dress, she stood before Jay. She was fully naked except for her feet, which were still protected by her red high heels.

Either the spotlight's brightness had increased, or the woman's skin had begun emanating some kind of a luminescence, because her features now appeared brighter and clearer than ever, so much so that their surroundings turned dimmer.

With nothing to conceal them anymore, her supple curves looked sharper and shapelier.

Jay wished he could look away, but he was transfixed by the enticing woman.

She had all the physical attributes that he found attractive in a woman. She had a thin, long neck. Her breasts were round and firm. They were neither too big, nor too small. Her brown nipples stood erect, as if they were beckoning Jay for a touch. Her flat belly had a light, but noticeable dent that ran from the bottom of her navel to a triangular mat of thin, shiny, black hair. Jay's eyes, disregarding his attempts to tear them away from the woman, devoured her from top to bottom.

Jay felt as if he were put inside a freezer. His stomach felt queasy, and his teeth chattered uncontrollably. The web shook along with his violently shivering body. His hands and feet were so cold that they hurt with a throbbing pain.

Amidst all the pain and uneasiness, there emerged a new feeling.

A feeling of nakedness.

And Jay saw that he was not wearing any clothes either.

He could not recall what he had been wearing all this time, or if he had been wearing anything at all. Stuck on a giant spider web in the middle of nowhere, the thought of his clothes had not crossed his mind. It was unimportant. But with his bare skin exposed to the creature and the lady and all the other prying eyes, he thought about his clothes. He felt ashamed. He felt scared.

They're watching.

He wanted to cover himself up, but with what, and how? His clothes had disappeared, and he could not move. Whatever was left of his free will had been confiscated from him. And now, stripped naked by the invisible arms, he was being subjected to a humiliation that would be too coarse a punishment for even the enemies of the Federation.

But why was he being punished?

He knew he was not the only naked human being there, but he could not see any discomfort or unease in the woman's face. She was smiling, as if she were enjoying Jay's distress.

Perhaps she was an android. Maybe he was abducted by the Underground Army, and the woman was there to show him what his kind had created and then refused to accept as an equal. Now it was their turn to treat him like a disposable machine.

And if she was a human being working for the Federation, then perhaps she was there to prove a point before beginning the experiments: he could not retaliate. And although in appearance they seemed to be in the same condition, their ranks in the Federation's system created a concrete distinction - they were both naked, but she was naked willingly, whereas Jay was not. She had a choice. He had none. She could put on her clothes again if she wanted to. He could not. She worked **with** the Federation. He worked **for** the Federation.

Android or human, there was no sign of insecurity or fear in her eyes.

Why'd she be scared?

She's free. I'm not.

"Still don't recognize me?" she said.

Jay shut his eyes.

(Spiders crawling. Red lights flashing. Voices talking in unison. Glasses clinking. Cobwebs. Disco. Jazz. Rock and roll. Cars stuck on a spider web. A throbbing sensation between his legs. A whisper: "I want you." A spider crawling on the bed. A damaged air conditioner. "Animals!" "We should go on a holiday." Yellow skies. A man with the head of a spider. "I love you.")

Fuck!

He opened his eyes.

He finally found the answer.

Looking the woman in the eyes, Jay shook his head. "No," he said. "No."

(Gasps and jeers.)

The smile disappeared from the woman's face. She stared hard at Jay. It seemed like she was waiting for him to say something more. But Jay had said all that he had to. He looked away.

Seconds. Minutes. Hours seemed to pass like that.

The two eyes on his left, the eight eyes on his right, and the numerous eyes hidden in the darkness all around him, observed the scene in complete silence.

Jay was thirsty. He looked at the floating glass. It was empty.

Finally, the woman let out a sigh, and slowly turned around.

With that movement, the spotlight was turned off, and the sounds were turned on again. The jazz music and the whispering voices were back.

But his clothes did not return. He was still naked.

The woman, too, was naked. She was standing the same way he had first seen her there – with her back turned towards him.

She brushed her long, black hair aside, exposing her back.

It was almost entirely covered with a large tattoo.

At first, the tattoo appeared like an abstract design. But after a few moments had passed, it resembled

no no no no no no no

a human face.

And although Jay could not recognise the woman, he had no difficulty in recognizing the face tattooed on her back.

There was no room for any kind of confusion because he had never forgotten that face. Although locked inside a vault in an impenetrable corner of his mind along with the rest of his secrets, that particular piece of memory always turned up to remind him of a weakness he tried so hard to get over.

Yes, it was *that* face.

The wailing face he had seen on an infernal spider's body twenty-eight years ago.

He felt a constriction in his throat. His stomach turned over. He felt as if several feet were stomping away on his chest.

The woman, without looking back at Jay, walked away. Towards the darkness.

And the web resumed its swinging again

Jay turned his head to the other side. The glowing eyes were getting bigger.

They were coming closer.

He gasped. That was all he could do with his sandpapered throat. The wet feeling on his legs was spreading.

Spreading all over his body.

He looked back at the woman retreating into the dark. The screaming face on her back was glowing.

He understood a bit of what was happening. The farther the woman was getting away from him, the closer the monster was moving in.

The voices were getting louder by the moment, and the jazz music was getting distorted. It sounded as if a damaged record was being played at full volume.

"You can stop it, Jay," a voice yelled out.

"You can stop it. You can stop it. You can stop it." Chanted several other voices.

"It's getting closer," another voice whispered in Jay's ear. "Stop her!"

No! No, I can't!

"You have to!"

No!

The web swung violently with slow, strong, steady rhythms. It was only a matter of time before the monster would come out of the dark.

"Do it, Jay!"

"Too late," whispered a voice, and all the voices stopped talking.

The lady disappeared into the darkness.

And a pair of massive pillars covered with dark brown fur and spikes emerged from the darkness on his right.

Jay immediately turned his face the other way.

How? How is this happening?

Gathering all his strength, Jay tried to wrench his limbs out of the web. He pushed and pulled and squirmed. But the webs were strong. They were like barbed wire. They dug into his flesh. It was extremely painful, but he did not stop struggling.

Even if the web cuts through my arteries and kills me, it'll still be better than being eaten by that thing.

All of a sudden, the space above him was filled with hundreds of swinging disco balls.

The balls were not glowing. They were also not floating anymore, but were hanging by thin wires.

Webs?

Jay understood what they were.

They were eggs!

Spider eggs!

Lifting up his torso, he shook himself. The webs around his wrists and ankles cut into his flesh, but he continued to squirm violently, trying to free himself.

Meanwhile, the spider's head had come out of the dark. Jay knew that looking at it would not be helpful at a time like this. But it was already too late. The spider had entered into his field of view, and he could not help but look.

Compared to its body, the spider's head was smaller in size. Three pairs of glowing eyes were looking directly at Jay. Another pair, placed at the sides of its head, was looking elsewhere. Under the frontal eyes hung two enormous fangs, which opened and closed with a clink.

Jay felt so weak that he stopped moving. He had seen enough to make him lose his mind. It was a miracle that he had not lost his consciousness yet. A scream tried to come out of his gut, but he channelled the energy towards his limbs instead. He tried bringing them together with all his strength. He could feel his flesh getting sliced off, but he kept tugging at the webs.

The spider, if it wanted to, could have already reached Jay, spun its web around him, sunk its fangs into his flesh, and liquefying his insides, turned him into spider food. However, it was taking its time. It was stopping every now and then, observing him.

But why?

(Crack!)

He heard a soft crackling sound.

(Crack! Crack! Crack!)

The eggs! They're hatching!

From somewhere far away, the old psychiatrist Dr Ray's voice drifted into Jay's ears.

"You have to face your fears."

But-

Something fell on Jay's belly.

It was a spider the size of a house cat.

Another one landed on his left leg.

Jay wiggled and shook himself, but the spiders stuck to him.

The one on his belly, baring its fangs, started crawling towards his face.

Screaming without a sound, Jay tugged harder.

Another spider fell on his right arm.

(*Harder.*)

And another.

(*Harder.*)

FUCK!

The webs finally snapped.

And Jay, free from the clutches of the cobweb, plummeted into the dark abyss.

He flailed his arms and legs, expecting to grab on to something. But there was nothing, except the spiders raining from above. Their hairy bodies brushed against his fingers.

He was falling into the darkness. Into the nothingness.

(*Falling.*)

The air was getting warmer

(*Falling.*)

and warmer.

(*Falling.*)

He could feel blisters bubbling up on his skin.

He felt them bursting.

The hysterical laughter of a woman filled up the air, deafening him as he fell through the bottomless perdition.

With a start, Jay opened his eyes, and shut them immediately as the daylight burned into his retinas.

The darkness was not pitch-black anymore.

The air was cool. It smelled of the tuberose-flavoured air freshener used in his house, of disinfectants, and of smoke. It tasted of copper and dust. The Song of the City was playing again. There was no other music in the air.

He moved his arms; his wrists were free. He moved his legs; his ankles were free. He touched the velvety bed sheet beneath him. There were no webs around; there was no abyss below.

Jay held his breath as he felt those familiar sensations, afraid that exhaling would make them go away.

But he knew he was safe. He was home.

He was awake.

He could breathe again. The polluted air had never felt so good.

He was alive. Conscious again.

But this meant he had just had a nightmare. He had dreamt.

And that connoted trouble.

Dreaming was an obsolete human function. It was eradicated by the Federation. A census, conducted three years ago, showed that only seven per cent of the world's total population dreamt regularly, although most of them could not remember what they dreamt of. They could only recall bits and pieces of their dreams, such as random images and sounds. All the dreamers were found to be between the ages of thirty and sixty. The people less than thirty years of age had never dreamt (and could never dream), whereas it was difficult to study the sexagenarians, as they suffered from dementia.

The Federation then decided to cure the people of their illness – the illness of dreaming. According to them, conscious dreaming or "thinking" was admissible, but subconscious dreaming was unnecessary, and to a large extent, dangerous. Evidently, it had been witnessed throughout history that dreams, directly or indirectly, provided people with the motivation to follow ridiculous ideas and carry out inimical stratagems, which always hindered the world's peace and security.

After the census was taken, Jay was listed amongst the "Dreamers." All the men and women belonging to that age group were made to participate in several experiments where the government scientists studied their brain functions and anatomy. That was an exhausting experience for Jay. Throughout the course, he had to run from one centre to another, participate in frivolous activities, and get his head shoved inside all sorts of machines. Luckily, even the most dexterous physicians and scientists could not find a trace of his ameliorated arachnophobia. And he did not feel the necessity to let them know anything about it.

After sixty days, the doctors shook his hand, and handed him a memo that said he was cured – he would never dream again. Nevertheless, he and all the other patients had to sign a contract that obligated them to report to the Society of Peacekeeping in case there was an unfortunate circumstance of dreaming.

And now, for the first time in over three years, Jay had dreamt.

Doing so, he induced a glitch in the sleep experiments, which the scientists had believed to be successful. As far as he knew, none of the cured "Dreamers" ever dreamt again. Following the pact, he would now have to report to the Society of Peacekeeping about it. Once again, he would have to go through all the ludicrous procedures. The other people who were listed with him would probably get called up as well. Jay did not want to be a part of this. He also *could not* disclose the contents of his nightmare. Thus, he made up his mind: he was not going to inform the Federation about any of this. That would be a breach of contract, but nobody would get to know about it if he kept his mouth shut.

And he knew he could keep it shut.

He crammed the incident into the little vault in his mind.

He knew it would be safe there.

But was *he* safe?

He opened his eyes.

He saw a white ceiling. There were no disco balls hanging from it. No eggs. It was the same ceiling that he saw every morning as he prepared his mind and body for a hectic day at the office.

He turned onto his side. The bed was empty. Propping himself up on his elbow, he rubbed the big, prickly dust off the corner of his eyes, and squinted at the closed bathroom door. The latch was open, which meant Sunita was inside.

With the spider.

But that was not going to be a problem. It was only a little house spider. Sunita was not afraid of spiders.

Or was she?

Just like Jay, she probably had her secrets. He grimaced at that notion.

The nightmare had already shaken him, and he did not want any other thought to mess up his mind early in the morning. He had a long day ahead of him.

A long day. Another long day at the office. Another ten hours in that cramped room, amidst the raucous city, surrounded by large piles of fat folders, with snoopy eyes observing every movement through the CCTV cameras installed in every corner of the office. And to top it all off, the air conditioner was damaged.

"Oh, shit!" Jay thought. "Tapas!" He should have called the mechanic last night, but the plan had completely escaped his mind.

He looked at the clock. Quarter to seven – still too early to make a phone call to a working class man.

Working class man: Jay pondered over the term.

Where's the line drawn between a working class man and a middle class man? The only difference between the postal worker Jay and the mechanic Tapas was that of capital. Jay had a larger income, an apparently steadier job, and a bigger house. Tapas lived away from the city, worked independently, and could go on holidays whenever he wanted to. Both, however, in different ways, were slaves to the same system designed by the Federation. Who, then, had the upper hand here?

But the line, wherever it was drawn, was essential for the existence of the State.

Eight years ago, the Federation had planned the establishment of a classless society, which led to the passing of the infamous Equal Works Act. The economy soon collapsed, and there were riots everywhere. Allegedly, thousands of people lost their jobs, and several hundreds died of hunger and poverty. Although the number of deaths was later corrected by the Federation after the abrogation of the act, the defectiveness of the idealized egalitarian society was witnessed first-hand by the entire world.

It was then that the citizens were classified into three classes: Upper, Middle, and Working. As a result of this, the Workers Party Association was founded, and on their demand, the Workers' Colonies were set up in every city. Almost all the working class people moved to the colonies, separating their household from the upper and the middle class people. Since then, there had been no cases of riots and deaths because of unemployment or poverty.

"This is the perfect society," the President had said. Everybody agreed.

Jay's temples were throbbing slightly. It was probably due to dreaming after such a long time. His brain had explored prohibited grounds. And now he would have to pay the price. But having to deal with an annoying headache was far better than volunteering for another brain-probing session.

His joints cracked as he sat up.

He imagined how Sunita would look as she came out of the bathroom. Although he had witnessed this numerous times over the years, it was one of the things he could never get tired of. Every time he saw her, he felt a pleasant warmth in his chest.

There was a soft rustle and a click; and the door swung open.

Jay felt the familiar warmth again.

But not the pleasant one in his chest.

No

It was the wet one on his legs.

His heart jumped into his throat.

It can't be

His jaw dropped onto the floor.

It can't be!

A gigantic spider was standing at the bathroom door. Its entire body was covered with thick, brown fur. It stood still, waving its pedipalps, staring at Jay with its eight black, beady eyes.

Jay's head was spinning like a carousel. ***Another dream?***

But he could hear the song of the city. He could taste the coppery air. He was in his house. In his bedroom. On his bed.

It's no dream!

Neither Jay nor the spider made any movement. His limbs had frozen solid.

Several minutes passed this way. Finally, the spider moved a hairy leg forward. With that, Jay's fight-or-flight response kicked in. He sprung back, and rolled over to the other side of the bed. He did all that without taking his eyes off the creature for even a single moment.

As if surprised by this sudden movement, the spider immediately drew back its leg.

Did the spider find its way out of my dream?

No. It was not the same spider. This spider was as big as Jay; the one in his nightmare was way bigger. It would not have fit inside the room.

But how could something escape a dream and get into the real world?

Was that even possible?

But then he was looking at a *giant spider inside his house*. How was *that* possible?

Oh, shit! The spider in the bathroom? Jay tried to draw a conclusion. Finding some kind of a conclusion for the time being, however fantastical it might be, was necessary for bringing his thoughts into order. But it was difficult, with all the questions and thoughts in his mind.

The spider from the bathroom. How did it grow so big?

An anomaly?

Or...

A drop of sweat trickled down Jay's forehead and entered into his right eye.

... an experiment?

Either way, he knew that the price was already paid. **Sunita**. She was nowhere to be seen.

Jay clutched his throat, where he felt the violent drumming of his heart. Momentarily, the spider and everything else around it became a blur.

I can't scream why can't I scream am I still dreaming

Did Sunita get the chance to scream?

No. He never heard her.

He only heard the screams of the city.

It never stopped screaming.

And it would never stop.

A drop of tear ran down his face. (Or was it sweat?)

I've lost everything.

(Everything?)

No. Not everything.

Ginny!

He wiped his tears (sweat?). Was Ginny okay? If the spider was locked inside this bathroom all this time, it could not have caused Ginny any harm, since she had her own little bathroom joined to her room.

There was a good chance that she was still in her room, probably asleep, unaware of what was going on. But safe.

And Jay had to save his daughter while he still could.

The giant spider in front of him was standing like a statue, ogling him. The bedroom door was only a few steps away, but the spider could reach it before him. He would have to act fast. But how could he move faster than a spider?

He tried to picture what he would have to do. The door was closed. He would have to open it without giving the spider the opportunity to pounce on him. Time was of the essence. He would have to keep moving. The slightest mistake would cost him the life of his daughter.

I couldn't save Sunita. But I can still save Ginny. I have to!

He clenched his fists to stop his hands from shaking.

"You have to face your fears," said the voice of Dr Roy.

Taking his cue from that, Jay dashed towards the door. He heard the spider hiss, and saw it scuttle across the room. But before it could reach him, he grabbed the door's handle, swung around the stile, and got out of the room. Shutting the door closed, he slid the latch.

All this happened within mere seconds. From the other side, the spider banged on the door. Jay was out of breath. His body was not cooperating with him. But there was not another moment to be wasted. With wobbly legs, he rushed into Ginny's room.

"Gi-"

No!

The little bed was empty.

Jay felt as if his heart would spring out of his chest.

Please.

The door of the little bathroom was slightly parted.

Please. Please. Please. Please.

He pushed open the door.

And a loud grunt came out of his mouth.

That grunt used the last bit of energy his body had retained. His legs buckled, and he collapsed on the floor.

A large, hairy, eight-legged creature was sitting on the toilet seat.

Another spider.

This spider was smaller than the one locked in his bedroom, but not any less intimidating.

A bathroom. A commode. A horrific spider.

It seemed like Jay was witnessing an exaggerated recreation of that one ignominious scene from his childhood, which, twenty-eight years ago, had triggered his arachnophobia, and had, since then, subjected him to a lifetime of unpleasant recollections.

The only thing missing was the face. Where was the face?

And where was Ginny? Could she have escaped somehow? The windows were girdled. But the door-

The spider jumped down from the toilet seat, baring its long, sharp fangs at Jay. He sprang up from the ground

(*Papa!*)

and noticed a pair of pyjama pants lying on the bathroom floor.

(*Papa! Can I play on your phone?*)

Ginny's pyjama pants.

Clutching his hair, he screamed.

Finally, the scream was successful. It was not inaudible anymore.

The Song of the City was momentarily stifled by Jay's screaming voice. And in that little moment, he tried to come to terms with the harrowing fact that his entire family was gone. **Dead.** But he could not wrap his head around it. Too many voices were screaming inside his head.

The sudden vocal eruption seemed to agitate the spider. Hissing, it jumped back to the corner of the bathroom.

The spider in the other room banged on the bedroom door even louder.

All this time, Jay had been worrying about his family. With them gone now, he at last thought about himself. He was locked inside a house with not one, but **two** giant spiders. Man-eaters. And he only knew about the presence of those two spiders because he had seen them. There could be more, hiding, waiting for him in the other rooms.

What would a man do now? Fight these monsters? And how would he do that? Using a weapon?

(Give them what they deserve. Avenge your family.)

But it's not gonna bring them back.

(It doesn't matter. Do the right thing. Kill them.)

I'm scared.

(They killed your family!)

Closing his eyes, Jay saw the faces of Sunita and Ginny floating before him. Slowly, they faded away. He felt a stabbing pain in his chest. It was excruciating. It was so intense that it overpowered every other feeling.

Including the wet feeling on his legs.

Jay looked down. His legs had stopped shaking.

He also saw something lying near his foot.

A home-cricket bat.

He picked it up.

He remembered the few times he had played home-cricket with his daughter. He never really liked this sport. A steel bat, a cotton ball, and a closed room – those were its only requirements. It seemed like a parody of cricket – a sport that he enjoyed so much growing up. Everything he enjoyed, everything he liked, everything he loved, was gone. Taken away from him.

He looked at the bat in his hand. Memories.

(*I'm very tired, baby. I'll play tomorrow.*)

His grip around the bat tightened.

"I'll fuck you up," he said through gritted teeth. He looked directly at the spider, and yelled, "I'll fuck you up! You hear me? I'll beat you to a pulp. I'll fucking-"

The next series of events occurred in a matter of seconds.

Baring its fangs with a hiss, the spider leapt off the ground. The moment Jay noticed its legs bending, he knew something bad was about to happen. He fell down on the carpeted floor just in time, ducking the spider, which jumped over him, landed on the floor, and scurried out of the room.

He followed the spider, clutching the bat with his sweaty palms.

As soon as he stepped out of the room, however, his grip around the bat's handle loosened. With a thud, the bat fell down on the floor.

The spider had opened the latch of the bedroom door.

He felt the warm wetness on his legs again. Has it ever gone away?

No.

It was there. It was always there.

I can't do this.

Turning around, he darted towards the front door.

Picking up all the keys from the key bowl, he opened the door latches with clumsy hands. He heard hissing and shuffling noises behind him, but he did not look back. Pulling the door open, he jumped outside, slammed the door shut, and locked it with the key.

Instantaneously, the spiders thumped and banged on the door. A second's delay would have been disastrous.

Jay's throat felt dry, and he started coughing. He was not wearing his gas mask.

Dark clouds were covering the sky. The sun was nowhere to be seen. It felt like the air had turned solid. It was like breathing in wet concrete.

Could he survive in this atmosphere without a mask?

We'll see.

He checked the keys he had picked up. Two sets of the house keys – his, and Sunita's. There was another pair of spare keys, but were the spiders intelligent enough to look for them in the wardrobe?

He stepped away from the door, and looked at his house. From the outside, it still looked beautiful. But only Jay, who had been inside, knew what its walls were sheltering.

He had hurried out of the house shirtless, mask-less, barefooted, and without any money. Now he did not know where to go from here. He did not even have his car.

He reached into his trouser pockets, half-expecting to find his mobile phone, despite knowing that it still was in the house, lying on his bedside table.

Not that the phone would have been helpful anyway. Whom would he call? The police?

If the spiders were indeed runaways from a government facility, then Jay would be taken in as a witness to a failed experiment. Or even worse, he would be detained as a witness to the product of a **successful** experiment. They could also be biological weapons, in which case, he would be in deeper waters. The Federation would never allow him to roam freely with that kind of information. The police would either take him away, or tactically erase him.

There was only one person who could help him now. Soumik.

He made it for Soumik's house next door.

Soumik worked at the data correctional department. It was a night job, so he slept during the day. Waking him up at this hour would be bothersome, but there was nobody else Jay could trust right now. He knew he would be risking Soumik's safety by indulging him in this abnormal affair, but something had to be done, and it could not be done alone. Also, Soumik lived alone; he would not have to worry about anybody else's safety if he got involved in Jay's preternatural predicament.

Jay rang the doorbell over and over again, until he heard movements inside.

He tried to collect the proper words for narrating the incident to Soumik. But was there any proper way to do that? And what if he did not believe him?

Well, we can always go in.

But go in there *again?*

The door creaked open.

"Soumik! I-" Jay could not finish his sentence. He had to gasp for breath.

A gigantic black spider was standing in front of him.

They got him too!

Without waiting another moment, Jay did a quick about-turn, and scrammed out of there.

Stepping out onto the street, he saw another huge spider strolling on the pavement. It walked right past him without even acknowledging his presence. Hearing a shuffle behind him, Jay saw that the spider from Soumik's house was speeding towards him.

He took to his heels again. As he whizzed past the spider on the pavement, it stopped and stared at him.

There were spiders of various sizes and colours all over the place. Standing in front of the houses, in the lawns, crawling on the street – they were everywhere. Numerous eyes gazed at the frantic man running barefoot and shirtless through the streets of Maxwell Corner. Jay was accustomed to the feeling of being under the constant surveillance of hidden, prying eyes. Probably the entire nation had gotten used to that by now. But as he found himself in a situation where he knew whom the eyes belonged to, he realised that he would have rather preferred the obscurity. It was better to live in utter ignorance than to live with a cognizance so terrifying.

"It is imperative for the people of the country to be knowledgeable," the President had once said. "But we must not get carried away. Do not let knowledge get the better of you. We humans should control knowledge. Knowledge must not control us. Remember this – knowledge is the most dangerous weapon of all. It has been used as a weapon in the past, and it will be used as a weapon in the future. Therefore, we must always be wise in our quest for attaining knowledge, and be careful about how we use it."

Soon after that, a worldwide research, funded by the Federation, was carried out by hundreds of scholars who had realised the truth of the statement. The research lasted for five years, during which time millions of books were passed through the correctional incinerators. Some of those books were held in high regard by the people, but the scholars provided them with appropriate reasons. "We do not need outdated philosophical and religious texts from thousands of years ago," they said. "We have to be progressive, and these texts are preventing us from moving forward." The people had to agree that they were living in darkness with a false sense of reality and hope propagated by the philosophical and religious books. And so they willingly threw their holy books into the fire.

They disowned God with ease because they chose to believe that God did not exist.

They accepted the Federation because the Federation was real.

While God's existence was purported by texts written by "vagabonds," "dreamers" and "pseudoscientists," the Federation's existence was purported by the Federation itself. Who then, was the superior entity?

God was omnipotent, omnipresent and omniscient in theory.

The Federation was all that in reality. All that, and more.

But now, running through the streets, past the monstrous spiders, Jay had nothing and nobody to turn to. He did not even know where he was going.

He only kept running.

He assumed that the Maxwell Corner Army Station was probably attacked by now, as it consisted of inept soldiers. It was common knowledge that the territorial troopers were actually interns from higher educational institutions, and unemployed men from middle class families. Anyone trying to earn a few extra world dollars could join the Territorial Army after taking the Common Phys Ed Examination. Even Deputy Manoj Suri, the art school dropout who could not even hold a paintbrush, could be seen walking around with a loaded rifle under his arm, eating hamburgers, and taking naps at the canteen.

It was at the heart of the metropolis, where the song of the city was the loudest, the air the filthiest, and the water the dirtiest, that the actual, academy-trained army personnel were deployed. Home to all the major institutes, industries and upper class people, it had to be properly guarded all the time. The armed forces never ran out of members, and so there were plenty of soldiers in the heart of the city. Joining the armed forces was a matter of great pride, as it guaranteed a proper job security, and the flow of regular paychecks. It also did not come with any serious dangers, being directly connected to the Federation, and having nobody to protect the country from. As per the One World Act, any country or countries trying to engage in warfare would be totally obliterated by the Society of Peacekeeping, and the grounds on which they stood would be used for agricultural purposes and nuclear research. Thus, the armed forces' only concern was to ensure the safety of the townsfolk, and their primary threat was the Underground Army.

The sounds of the automobiles and the recorded advertisements were getting louder with every step now.

Jay finally reached the thoroughfare that would lead him out of the neighbourhood.

This connecting passageway was a narrow one. It allowed only one car to pass at a time. Being the only short cut to the heart of the city, it was always kept unoccupied. The traffic light at the terminal marked the end of Maxwell Corner, and the entryway to the heart of the city.

But Jay had to stop.

The thoroughfare was blocked.

It was entirely clogged with spider webs.

It was not an ornate orb web, but a mesh of messy tangled webs running from one wall to another.

Jay had only one alternative, which was to take the longer route to the main city. But that route would take him over five hours even if he used a car. Jay did not have his car, and he could not even borrow one from his neighbours, as it was very certain that none of them were alive anymore.

He saw that a few spiders had gathered behind him, blocking the road. They did not appear hostile, but their presence meant that there was no going back now. He *had* to move to the heart of the city.

But what'd I do then?

Through the small gaps between the webs, Jay saw the traffic light turn green.

Now!

Shielding his face with his arms, he hauled himself onto the mesh of webs.

He only managed to move a few steps forward, after which his legs got entangled in the cobwebs. He was about to fall face first onto the concrete, but he clutched on to the webs sticking to his arms, and secured his poise. Freeing his arms, he tried to remove the webs from around his ankles. But he could not get them off. They clutched onto his legs, shoulders, and back, holding him back as if they were several pairs of hands. Fortunately, Jay managed to keep his face protected from the webs. He looked behind once to see if the spiders were following him. To his surprise, they were still standing on the other side of the street, eyeing him with their grotesque, expressionless faces.

But he knew that sooner or later, they would get to him.

Every single step that he took increased his difficulty to move ahead. Using all his strength, he dragged himself forward, pulling the cobwebs along with him. But he made sure to not make any random, hasty movement because he knew that struggling would only cause him to get ensnared by the webs.

Gotta... keep... moving...

He could now see the cars and the buses on the main street.

Almost there. Almost-

The traffic light turned red with a resounding beep. Jay stumbled forward as the webs snapped, detaching themselves from his body. It seemed like they had suddenly lost all their strength and adhesiveness. But he was free at last. He looked back at the cobwebs he had left behind. The strands of web swirled in the air like drops of ink dropped in water.

He was now only a couple of steps away from entering into the heart of the city. He could hear it beating. The rushing automobiles looked full of life and vigour. They were always livelier and more vigorous than the ones who operated them.

After removing the last pieces of cobweb sticking on to his body, he felt even more naked. The fact that he would have to walk the streets of the metropolis this way made his skin crawl.

He recalled his colleagues' remarks from the previous evening:

"Look at that hick. Doesn't even have a shirt on!"

"Who doesn't have fuckin' clothes?"

"Maybe working class men?"

"They don't walk around naked. Even *they* have some dignity."

Dignity.

Would anybody even give him a lift? **Absolutely not.** Maybe the working class people would pity his condition? **Maybe.** Or would they laugh in his face, and enjoy his suffering? **Possible. Everything's possible in City-8.**

But one thing was for sure: nobody cared for a man without clothes.

Jay had to take advantage of the negligence the mysterious "street-walkers" were subjected to. Maybe he could escape the police and the Territorial Army by assuming the appearance of one of those street-walkers. But he knew that all the people would be staring at him with disgust. And what about those invisible eyes that followed him everywhere? Could he ever escape them? Could he ever hide from them?

Turning to the left, he stepped on to the road verge. The moment he did so, his heart skipped a beat. His legs lost balance, and he slumped down onto the artificial grass.

The bus stand stationed at the verge, as always, was crowded.

But not with people.

It was crowded with spiders.

A bus with blackened windows pulled over. Its door opened with a hiss. Some of the spiders crawled into the bus, while the others remained back. The door closed with a beep, and the bus drove off.

Jay looked at the road.

It was jammed with cars and motorbikes. Almost all the cars had blackened windows, so he could not see the drivers. But he could clearly see the ones riding the motorbikes.

Spiders. ***Spider-riders***. They were sitting on their huge hinds, using two of their frontal legs for holding the handlebars. They were even wearing helmets on their tiny heads.

A car stopped in front of a textile store on the other side of the road. A spider got out of the car, and crawled into the store.

Another bus arrived. This one had transparent windows. Through them, Jay saw that it was occupied by spiders. The remaining spiders from the bus stop boarded the bus. They wore blue caps bearing a picture of an axe – the symbol of the Workers Party Association. The bus sped away, leaving a trail of black smoke behind.

Jay was too shocked to think straight. It took him some time to get out of his bewilderment.

And then he finally realised what was going on.

Giant spiders had not invaded the world, nor had he entered into a world of spiders. Instead, all the human beings – the entire population – had turned into spiders.

Everyone except Jay.

"If I become somebody else," Sunita had asked him the previous morning, "will you still love me?"

"Yes," Jay had answered.

And then he locked his wife in their bedroom, and threatened to beat his daughter to death with a home-cricket bat.

But were they my wife and my daughter?

Or were they spiders?

He held out his hands before him. They looked like human hands. *His* human hands. He counted his fingers. *One. Two. Three. Four. Five. Six. Seven. Eight. Nine. Ten.*

He counted them again, this time backwards. But nothing changed.

It was the same Jay, in the same City-8, in the same world. Only the other residents of the world had changed their appearances. *But what about the animals?* Jay looked around. He saw a spider on the other side of the road, walking a dog on a leash.

So the animals are still here. What about the birds? He looked up at the sky.

He saw the zeppelins, the helicopters, and the dark clouds. There was no sky. There were no birds.

And what about the androids? They were not completely human. So, was it not possible that they did not turn into spiders? But where would he find them? And more importantly, why would they help him?

Jay was always lonely. He felt lonely when he sat for breakfast and dinner with his family, he felt lonely while commuting to the post office, he felt lonely while working in the office, and he felt lonely while sleeping with his wife. He never expected he could feel any lonelier than he already did. But as he sat alone on the artificial grass planted on a neglected verge of City-8, he discovered a new-found loneliness. It not only made him feel scared and miserable, but it also forced him into loosening his grip around his sanity. He could feel it in his bones, which were screaming for movement. He was in the heart of the city. Even the body did not permit any kind of inaction there. One had to keep moving.

Standing up, Jay started walking towards no specific destination.

The factory-manufactured trees and grasses gave the verge a morose appearance. The leaves, flowers, and benches were covered with dust. Although this side of the road worked as an unofficial limited-access road, every once in a while a pedestrian spider appeared on the pavement, probably en route to the bus stand. To avoid running into them, Jay walked on the padded ground. Nobody used the padded region for walking (or sitting), and so the grasses had become stiff and thorny. They pricked his calloused feet, but he kept walking.

There was no disruption in the usual ways of city life. The townsfolk were still walking, running, riding motorbikes, and driving cars. Two legs or eight, two hands or zero, they knew they had to keep working. They were programmed that way. And so the spiders were using their arachnid bodies as human bodies. Jay noticed that they were wearing masks made of web. The heavy gas masks were no longer needed. The former humans had already adapted to their physical changes, because although their bodies had changed, their responsibilities were still the same.

But what responsibilities did Jay have now? He was hurled out of the social hierarchy. As a member of the human society, he belonged to the middle class. But where would he fit into the *spider society*? There was no place for him in this society anymore. Now, there were upper class spiders, middle class spiders, and working class spiders. He would have to wait until the government introduced a separate class where he could fit in. But that too, would happen only if they decided to let him live. Unless there were a thousand other humans like him, the government would not care. Why would they? How could a puny human being be better than a spider? How could he ever outwork a spider?

He was helpless. He did not even have a place to go. The post office was the only refuge he could think of, but how would he get there? Even a working class spider would not give him a lift. And could he go back to his family after antagonizing them? Would they understand his perplexity? They belonged to a different species now. Could they think along the same lines?

And can I face them?

His house would be empty in a few hours. Sunita had to go to work, and Ginny had to go to school. Jay looked back at the road he had walked thus far. He could go back, put on some clothes, and think things over. However, he had caused a scene in the neighbourhood. Someone might have definitely informed the police. Maybe Sunita herself filed a report. But in that case, the post office would not be a safe place either. If the police caught him, what would he say to save himself? He would be tactically erased on the spot. Or worse, he would be taken to a research centre. Jay shuddered at the thought.

He reached the junction, where the verge ended. Now he had four directions to choose from. The city was spread before him like a massive cobweb. If he moved slowly, he would eventually be attacked and devoured by the spiders. If he moved fast, he would be smothered by the webs. There seemed to be no way out of there. No escape.

He had nowhere to go, nobody he could trust. He was all alone in the world. He was the only man in a world of spiders.

The road straight ahead would lead him to the Wild East Club. **No**. On the right was the road to his office. But he knew that the police would definitely look for him there. The road on the left was blocked with a tarpaulin. A sign before it read: "Caution: Road Work Ahead."

What should I do?

His question was answered with a blare of sirens.

Those whining sirens meant only one thing – the police were out on a hunt.

The traffic lights turned red. All the automobiles skidded to a halt. The pedestrian spiders, taking off their masks, froze on the pavement.

The protocol was that whenever the emergency siren would be heard, every activity on the road had to stop. The car windows had to be rolled down, the gas masks had to be removed, and the pedestrians had to kneel on the ground, putting their hands behind their heads, so that the police could carry out their biotech scanning properly. Not following this protocol led to a fine of five thousand world dollars, and the removal of a finger. Everybody, therefore, always happily obliged. The police would then use their biotech scanners on every single human, animal, and automobile in the area for recognizing whoever they were after. This was necessary because the police were always very careful about the safety of the citizens.

But in this case, the biotech scanners would not be necessary. Their eyes would be enough. Jay was the only human being in the city.

Or maybe in the whole world. Maybe the planet itself had turned into one gigantic spider crawling around the sun, weaving a web.

He had to hide.

But where?

He stepped behind the polystyrene bark of a tree on the verge. He believed that it would be a comparatively safer place to hide, as nobody, not even the police, ever looked at the trees.

Surprisingly, the police still carried on their search with the biotech scanners. Holding his breath, Jay listened to the Song of the City, the blare of the sirens, the soft cluttering of hundreds of spider feet, and the incessant beeping and buzzing of the biotech scanners.

The sounds were getting closer. Closer. Closer.

Jay peeped from behind the tree trunk.

A spider wearing a police cap was aiming a biotech scanner at the window of a huge white lorry parked directly in front of Jay. The scanner buzzed, indicating a negative identity.

The police spider suddenly turned around, looking directly at Jay.

His legs turned into water.

Time seemed to freeze as they stared at each other.

The spider had only taken one step towards him, when a deafening explosion rocked the ground.

Jay fell face-first on the ground. Bits and pieces of stones and gravel rained on him. Smoke and debris filled up the air. There was a loud whirring sound nearby.

After the smoke had cleared off, Jay saw several spiders lying on their backs with their legs curled up against their stiff bodies.

Something else had appeared amidst the carcasses and the wreckage – a huge car-like VTOL aircraft.

It had the letter "X" painted across its body.

The Underground Army!

The androids had attacked the police. And unknowingly, they had saved Jay.

The surviving police spiders, after resuscitating from their shock, blasted their machine guns at the aircraft.

But the Underground Army's VTOL aircraft remained unscathed. Its bulletproof surface rendered the guns useless.

Realising this, the police stopped firing.

Everything was perfectly still for an entire minute.

Was there hope?

But hope for what?

Jay held his breath.

Suddenly, the lid of the aircraft sprung open, and a black figure jumped out of it.

What the-

Eight legs. Two enormous pincers. A long, curved tail. A spearhead.

A stinger.

A scorpion!

The giant scorpion landed on top of one of the police spiders. Grabbing it with its massive pincers, the scorpion flung the spider on the ground, spilling its body fluids and internal organs all over the place.

Another scorpion jumped out of the aircraft. It lunged at a spider, impaling it with its spear-like stinger.

The scorpions began to rip apart the spiders' legs.

In a flash, an aircraft whooshed over them. An orange spider jumped down from it, and spat a whitish liquid at one of the scorpions. The liquid hit it on its face.

With a hissing sound, the scorpion's face melted away as if it were made of paraffin wax.

An unbearable stench filled up the air.

Jay retched.

What the fuck is going on here?

Spiders. Scorpions.

He was witnessing a battle.

A battle of the arachnids.

He had to get out of there.

Crawling on his elbows and knees, he made for the blocked road. He scooted under the tarpaulin, leaving the bloody battlefield behind.

Due to an ongoing large-scale construction, the place was uninhabited. There were sacks of sand, cement, gravel, iron rods, and bricks lying around like discarded corpses. The air had turned grey with the construction dust. It reeked of cement and bricks, mixed with the smell of the arachnids' corpses.

Jay's nose was getting clogged with the dust. He coughed and wheezed. His feet, and the skin of his elbows and knees were lacerated. His sore legs refused to move any further. His stomach growled. He felt as if he were walking through a furnace. But he kept dragging himself forward.

The construction works for the day had not begun yet. He was all alone there.

Tall, colourless and windowless buildings loomed over Jay like a crowd of titans witnessing a street play. Jay read the signs outside the buildings: "Under Construction," "Keep Out," "Danger," "Property Of...," "Men at Work." *Men at work? Or spiders at work?*

He wondered what the spiders would look like working with the instruments and tools that were originally designed for humans.

He finally came across a building without a sign. It was a two-storey building, painted grey. Or maybe it was whitewashed and the dust had turned it grey.

There were no bags of cement, or piles of stone chippings in the vicinity of the building. It looked like its construction work was complete. A short flight of stairs led to an ornate portico, which was a clear indication that the building belonged to some upper class person. (Or spider.) Thick layers of dust had settled in the passageway and on the door. Although that was not a solid proof of the place being uninhabited, as it would only take a couple of minutes for the dust to settle like that, there was no way that an upper class person would move in there when the surroundings were so noxious. They would definitely wait until all the construction works around them were over. The building was most possibly unoccupied, which meant there were no spiders inside.

But was the door open?

Jay's thoughts were interrupted by the rumble of a truck. It was coming his way. He sprinted up the stairs and grabbed the doorknob. Turning it around,

please-

He pushed the door.

It opened without a sound.

Rushing inside the house, Jay closed the door. It was painted white on the inside, and had a peephole. He looked through it, but saw nothing. The lens outside was covered with dust. Did they see him? Holding his breath, he listened to the truck. Without slowing down or stopping by the house, it drove away. Jay released his breath. And then, leaning his back against the door, he sat down on the floor.

It was a large room. The windowless walls, the high ceiling, and the cold floor were all painted white. They were not just whitewashed, but painted with a dazzling white paint. There were no hints of any other colour. Even a smudge of brick dust was nowhere to be seen.

There was a short passageway before Jay, which probably led to the other rooms.

Jay closed his smarting eyes. They felt heavy with all the dust that had settled in them.

The Song of the City and all the other noises were muffled inside the house. It seemed incredible that only a few metres away, a bloody battle was taking place between the former humans and the former androids. The walls were perfectly insulated. Could Jay install such noise-insulating walls in his house? Or was it a luxury reserved for the upper class people? But even if he could, what was the use? He could never set foot in his house again. He could never go home again.

Home. Where was it? At Maxwell Corner? In City-8? Or was there any other place he could call home? The post office? **No**. The world? **No**. The world was no longer his home. He was an intruder here. An intruder in the world of spiders and scorpions.

"God!" Jay silently called out. "God, are you there?"

But God did not answer.

"Do you see me, God?" Jay looked up at the white ceiling. "Won't you help me?"

Again, God remained silent.

Were the strong, soundproofed, whitewashed walls standing as a barrier between Jay's pleas and God?

Jay wondered what Sunita and Ginny would do without him. He wished he could imagine them being helpless without him, but he knew that they would be fine. They would carry on with their lives. The police, of course, would suspect them of hiding him somewhere. After all, they were his family; they would be expected to be loyal to him.

Loyal.

(*Do you recognize me?*)

Loyal.

But as responsible citizens, they would have to be loyal to the country first. What was the individual before the nation? Nothing.

"What if I surrender?" Jay wondered. "Will they let me live, then?"

His stomach answered the question with some loud growls.

He was terribly hungry. And thirsty. It was impossible to find food or water in this empty house. He would have to wait until it got dark so that he could sneak into one of the other buildings and search for some food and water left behind by the construction workers. But when would it get dark? He did not know what time it was.

Time. Running. Slipping away.

Who would win the battle: the spiders, or the scorpions? Jay did not care. In any case, there was no hope for him.

There's no light.

Jay closed his eyes and whispered, "Show me the light, God. Show me the light."

When he opened his eyes, he noticed that the far end of the short passageway appeared brighter.

Light?

Did God hear my prayers?

No. Ventilators.

Although he did not have any strength left in his body, he picked himself up from the ground. The chances of finding anything helpful in the other room were zero, and the ventilators would surely be too high up for him to look outside; but he dawdled through the passageway, wishing to be in the light.

The moment he stepped into the room, he stopped dead in his tracks.

It was an unusually large room. It was so expansive that it did not seem to be a part of the same house. Just like the first room, it was empty, and painted entirely white.

But it was washed with light.

And it was not uninhabited.

There was a giant spider in the room.

A tarantula?

It was standing a few yards away on Jay's left.

(A loud, deep, humming sound.)

Jay did not back off from the spider. There was something different about it.

Its eyes.

Jay could perceive the emotions in the spider's emotionless eyes.

They looked confused. And scared.

The man and the spider, facing each other, stood in the white room.

(Trumpets.)

Jay did not feel the warm wetness on his legs.

He heard a familiar tune.

A musical composition.

Richard Strauss's *Also sprach Zarathustra*.

He was not scared.

As if under a spell, he walked towards the spider.

And the spider walked towards him.

(*You have to face your fear.*)

Jay extended his arm, slowly getting closer to the spider.

The spider, as if it were imitating Jay, lifted one of its frontal legs, moving closer to him.

(Timpani.)

The fingers of the man and the claws of the spider reached out to one another.

(*You have to*)

And finally, Jay's fingers touched

(*face your fear.*)

the cold, hard surface of the mirror.

About the Author

Aditya Modak prefers to identify himself as a storyteller who weaves his ideas into stories that try to explore the absurdities of human life and existence, using words and images. Born and raised in Agartala, he spends his days reading books, watching films, and listening to classic rock albums. "Arachnid" is his authorial debut.

www.ingramcontent.com/pod-product-compliance
Lightning Source LLC
LaVergne TN
LVHW041851070526
838199LV00045BB/1537